ACCLAIM
TO CAPTURE A M
Book

"I loved the mix of adventure, romance, and faith in this delightful tale set in historic Yellowstone and Idaho. Isaiah Coltrane's strength and integrity made him a worthy hero for spirited Lady Amanda Whitcombe. Although their backgrounds couldn't be more different, they share a love for the natural beauty of the West and a genuine faith. Their inspiring story will take readers on an exciting and romantic journey they're sure to enjoy. Well written and highly recommended!" — Carrie Turansky, award-winning author of *A Token of Love* and *The Legacy of Longdale Manor*

"I love this book. From the very first chapter of *To Capture a Mountain Man*, it is a pleasure to encounter such a masculine man and feminine woman. He easily carries her to safety, and she is dwarfed but warmed by his jacket. Ahhh, the implied chivalry and physical contrast hint at future romance without throwing it in the reader's face. Spirited heroine Amanda Whitcombe is quickly intrigued by mountain man Isaiah Coltrane, as readers will be. The flow of Hatcher's story will pull you along as swiftly as the Yellowstone river that triggers this adventure in the first place." — Trish Perry, author of *Why She Never Told Me*

"Once again, Hatcher has brought vastly different characters from both sides of the Atlantic together and proven all things are possible. Readers will be drawn inexorably into their personal conflicts amid the dangers of the breath-stealing setting of our 19th century west from start to finish." — Linda Windsor, author of the Irish *Fires of Gleanmara* and Scottish *Brides of Alba* trilogies

"I was quickly caught up in this delightful 'opposites attract' romance, and enjoyed how author Robin Lee Hatcher developed the relationship between Isaiah and Amanda. Against the backdrop of the American West in the late 1800s, Hatcher blends together turn-the-page adventures — right up to the suspense-filled ending. As with all her novels, *To Capture a Mountain Man* includes an uplifting spiritual thread." — Beth K. Vogt, Christy Award-winning author

"I couldn't put down Robin Lee Hatcher's newest book, *To Capture a Mountain Man*. What a delightful read! Close to the turn of the twentieth century, rugged western mountain man Isaiah Coltrane has no idea his life will be turned upside down when he rescues spunky English tourist, Lady Amanda Whitcombe from drowning in a river in Yellowstone National Park. I fell in love with Isaiah and Amanda, and the spectacular scenery came to life as their adventures and mishaps kept me turning the pages and rooting for them to overcome the impossible circumstances that divided them." — Sunni Jeffers, author of romance, Americana, and Speculative fiction

"Another great story in Robin Lee Hatcher's delightful The British are Coming historical series. Set in 1895 in Yellowstone National Park and Idaho, this is the story of Lady Amanda Whitcombe and Isaiah Coltrane, the mountain man who finds her in the river. Forced together they try to deny their feelings for each other. But Amanda is an independent determined woman and Isaiah has more than met his match. A heartwarming story of the wild west and the men and women who conquered it together." — Lenora Worth, award-winning author

To Capture A Mountain Man

THE BRITISH ARE COMING
BOOK THREE

ROBIN LEE HATCHER

Paperback ISBN: 978-1-962005-08-1
eBook ISBN: 978-1-962005-07-4

Library of Congress Control Number: 2024927550

Published by RobinSong, Inc.
Meridian, Idaho

Chapter One

I saiah Coltrane squatted next to his buckskin gelding and studied the tracks on the ground. Looked like five horses and a couple of pack mules. Five poachers going deep into the Yellowstone backcountry. It was illegal to hunt in the national park but that didn't stop men like the ones he followed. They came for bison, elk, deer, wolves, and bears. They came for hides and antlers and meat. Although rather than getting caught, they would leave the meat to rot while they escaped with hides and other trophies.

He stood, his gaze following the trail until it disappeared into the dense forest.

Nearly ten years earlier, the U.S. Army had been brought in to help protect the park from illegal hunters. The soldiers' presence had reduced poaching incidents, but it hadn't eliminated them. Private game scouts like

1

Isaiah were still needed to track poachers, especially in the remotest areas of the park.

He took a deep breath of the cool, pine-scented air before putting his foot in the stirrup and settling into the saddle.

"Bandit!"

His black and white collie ran up from the creek, ready for whatever command came next.

"Let's find 'em."

Bandit sniffed the ground, then moved out ahead. Isaiah pressed his heels against Buck's sides, and the horse started after the dog.

Isaiah had been catching poachers in the park for the past three summers. He wasn't opposed to hunting wild game for food. He liked a good venison steak as well as the next man. But killing animals—especially the bison—in this park angered him. The American bison had, at one time, covered the West with a population in the tens of millions. But in this century, *his* century, the magnificent beast had been hunted to near extinction. Fewer than a thousand remained on the continent, and he was determined to do his part to help the bison survive and thrive again. Yellowstone National Park was one area of the country—perhaps the only one—where that could happen.

After Isaiah left the East at the age of nineteen, he'd stayed in a number of places along the way west. Colorado. Wyoming. Oregon. Washington. Idaho. But it was Montana where he'd settled at last. He'd built himself a log cabin north of the park, and there he'd remained, living the life that had called to him since he was a boy, sitting in his father's study, listening to his father's friend Jonas O'Brien telling about the mountain men and how they'd lived in harsh and lonely conditions in the first half of the century.

These mountains and valleys weren't as lonely in the closing decade of the nineteenth century. Americans from the East and immigrants from other nations had spread across the land, both before and after the War Between the States. But life remained hard, even harsh. It could be—

A gunshot broke into his thoughts. Instinctively, he reined in, his gaze sweeping the terrain at the same time he pulled his Winchester from its scabbard. The next sound he heard was a scream. A woman's scream.

"Haw!"

Buck broke into a gallop, Bandit leading the way. Isaiah leaned low, trying to avoid the tree branches that seemed determined to slap him in the face and sweep him from the saddle. Through the dense forest, he saw a clearing, the sun spilling a golden glow over the tall grasses. When he and Buck burst into the open, Isaiah glimpsed horses and riders disappearing into the trees across the clearing to his right. To his left, he saw an agitated horse, reins dragging on the ground, on the crest of the riverbank. He reined Buck to the left.

"Help!"

He saw her then, flapping her arms, struggling to stay afloat against the river's strong current. He pressed his heels into Buck's sides, and they raced along the bank to get ahead of the woman. Finding the right spot,

Isaiah vaulted from the saddle and slid down to the water's edge. He grabbed hold of a shrub with his right hand as he stepped into the icy river, reaching out in time to grasp the woman's water-sodden coat with his left hand. He felt fabric tearing and feared he would lose her.

God, help me.

Somehow, he got hold of her upper arm even as the current attempted to sweep her away. He tightened his grip—on her and the shrub—and hauled her toward the bank. Needles on the shrub pricked his right hand through his glove, and he grimaced against the pain as he drew the woman the final distance to the shore.

Still half in and half out of the water, he released her. She tried to crawl up the bank, coughing and choking. She only made it a couple of feet before she collapsed into a heap.

"Miss?" He leaned over, touching her shoulder. "Miss?"

There was no response.

He swept a wet mass of dark hair away from her face. Her eyes were closed, her expression slack, but she was breathing. She must have fainted. Quickly, he slipped both arms beneath her limp form and carried her to the top of the riverbank, where Buck and Bandit waited for him.

She was a slight thing, even with her clothes sopping wet, and it took little effort to carry her to a grassy area. He gently laid her on the ground, then straightened and took a step back. "Bandit."

The collie was at his side in an instant.

"We okay?"

Bandit raised his nose, sniffing the air. If the poacher who'd fired the shot remained nearby, the dog would warn him. But Bandit gave no sign of alarm.

Isaiah's attention returned to the unconscious woman. What was he supposed to do with her? How did she come to be out in this forest alone? Was she one of the poachers? That seemed unlikely. Even bedraggled, she looked too . . . refined.

And too pretty.

She groaned.

"Miss?"

She turned her head to the side and coughed again, spitting up river water.

He waited. One thing he'd learned over the past decade was patience. He needed it when hunting game to feed himself or when tracking poachers. Waiting never seemed a bad option.

Her coughing stopped, and she opened her eyes, blinking against the sunlight. After a long moment, she noticed him, gasped, and sat up.

He held out a hand. "It's all right, miss. I'm not here to hurt you. I pulled you from the river."

She glanced about, apparently not reassured.

"Bandit," Isaiah said softly.

The dog moved toward her, gave her a few sniffs, then licked her face. She gasped a second time. But after a few moments, she released a soft laugh. The most delightful sound he'd heard in ages.

"I'm Isaiah Coltrane. What's your name?" He waited for her answer.

AMANDA WHITCOMBE BLINKED AGAIN. Confusion fogged her thoughts, exacerbated by the exhaustion from her time in the water and a painful pounding in her head. She knew how to swim, but when her horse had thrown her into the rushing river, she'd hit her head on something. Something hard. A boulder, no doubt. Add to that fear—had one of those men she'd come upon actually fired a gun at her?—and it was no wonder her brain was muddled.

"Miss?"

"Did someone shoot at me? I . . . I . . . I don't know."

"You don't know who you are?"

Ridiculous question. She certainly knew who she was. Lady Amanda Whitcombe from England. Daughter of the Fifth Earl of Hooke, recently deceased. Sister to the Sixth Earl of Hooke, recently married and even now on his way to England with his American bride.

The man who'd rescued her frowned. Then he turned and walked to the buckskin gelding. He returned moments later with a canteen in hand. Staying an arm's length away, he squatted and held the canteen toward her. "You'd better have a drink."

She pushed herself into a sitting position. "I think I drank enough water already."

He smiled—and the power of it made her feel breathless for a different reason than near drowning.

"At least you didn't lose your sense of humor in the

river," he said, ending with a soft chuckle. Then he sobered. "How did you come to be out here by yourself?"

Amanda shook her head, not because she didn't know, but because she didn't want to return to that group of park tourists she'd been with for several days. One of the other women—Mrs. Johnson by name—had made it her job to tell Amanda what to do and what to say and what to eat. Not to mention her determination to pair Amanda with her pathetic son, Manford. Every day of the tour so far had been sheer torture.

She'd wanted to be left alone to enjoy the beauty of the park. To let nature heal the grief in her heart. Earlier today she'd had enough. She rode away from the wagons and horses, disappearing into the dense forest, wanting only a brief respite from the others. Before she knew it, she became disoriented. She'd called out but there'd been no answer.

"Miss, I believe you stumbled on some poachers I've been tracking. I'm guessing they fired a warning shot to scare you away. They could've shot you or your horse, but they didn't. You were lucky."

"Lucky?" Her voice cracked. "I went into the river and hit my head." She reached to touch the tender spot. "I could have drowned."

"Whatever your name, it's plain you aren't an American."

She nearly responded that, of course, she wasn't an American. But if she pretended she couldn't remember her name, she supposed she wouldn't remember where she was from.

She closed her eyes. *Tell him the truth. He must know the park if he's tracking poachers. He can get you wherever you need to go.*

She looked at him again. "I have forgotten your name."

"Isaiah. Isaiah Coltrane."

The name fit him. Isaiah Coltrane. Perfect for a man with such rugged good looks, one wearing a buckskin jacket. Like the mountain men of old. Like a younger version of Buffalo Bill Cody, only much more handsome with the shadow of a beard on his jaw and those piercing blue eyes.

Ignorant of her thoughts, he removed his jacket. "You're shivering, miss. You'd best take off that wet coat of yours." He waited until she followed his suggestion. Then he put his jacket around her shoulders.

It dwarfed her, but its warmth began to thaw her.

"Sit there and I'll get your horse."

Despite his instructions, Amanda pushed to her feet as soon as he turned his back. Her head continued to pound, and she winced beneath the pain even as she pulled Isaiah's coat closer around her. She watched as he approached her horse. The sorrel looked meek and mild now. The mare didn't shy away from him, didn't even lift her head to interrupt her grazing. There was no sign of the mount that had reared up in terror and thrown its rider into the river.

Isaiah took hold of the reins trailing on the ground, clucked, and led the mare toward Amanda. "Are you able to ride?"

"Dear me. Of course I can ride." She took a step

forward. Spots appeared before her eyes in wild array, and she felt the earth shift beneath her feet a moment before darkness swallowed her whole.

Chapter Two

This time, Isaiah caught the woman before she hit the ground. He glanced over at his collie. "Now what?"

Bandit barked once, then sat and watched his master, his expression seeming to say, *You caught her. You decide.*

Isaiah grunted in response. He supposed he'd have to make camp right around where they were. The poachers were long gone by now. One of them must have seen him ride into the clearing. They'd know he'd been on their trail but had stopped to rescue the woman, and they wouldn't delay putting plenty of distance between him and them.

His gaze fell to the woman in his arms. Pulling her from the river had cost him over a week of tracking. He'd been close. So very close. Still, God in His mercy had seen fit to have him arrive in time to keep her from drowning. That was of more importance than catching poachers.

With a sigh, he carried her along the bank of the river until he found a suitable campsite. Checking to be sure she was still breathing, he laid her in the long grass, then went back for the horses while Bandit stood guard. By the time he returned, his unnamed guest had begun to stir again.

"Oh, dash it all," she mumbled.

Isaiah stopped.

She sat up. "Did I faint again?"

"Yes, miss. You did."

She reached to touch the spot on the back of her head. "Ooh."

"Tender?"

"Yes."

He moved to stand behind her, leaning forward. There wasn't any blood. It had probably washed away in the river. He touched her head with his index and middle finger. A lump had risen on her scalp.

"Ouch!" She jerked away.

"Sorry. I should've asked first."

"Yes." She turned her head and glared up at him. "You should have asked." Her tone was imperious, dismissive, and there was more color in her cheeks now, along with a defiant spark in her chocolate brown eyes.

"I apologize." He stepped back, then walked to the mare. With an economy of movement, he soon had the horses unsaddled and unbridled. He hobbled them both, allowing them to graze. Then he made a fire and laid a blankct as close to it as was safe from sparks.

"Better warm yourself, miss. Try to get those clothes dry." He glanced at the sun, well past its zenith now.

"It'll be dark in a few hours and will get a whole lot colder than it is now. I'll try to hunt us up something to eat. My supplies are getting low." He drew his rifle from its scabbard.

"You're going to leave me here?" she asked, sounding less defiant now. "Alone?"

"Bandit will stay with you." He cocked an eyebrow. "Do you know how to shoot a gun?"

"I . . . I think so." She frowned, as if trying to pull up a memory.

Isaiah took his revolver from its holster and offered it to her, grip first. "Just be sure you don't shoot me by accident when I return."

"I am not a fool, Mr. Coltrane." Her pert nose rose in the air, and stubbornness set her jaw.

He wanted to ask how she would know that if she didn't even know her name or how she came to be there. But decided better of it. "Just being cautious."

Rather than reply, she lowered her head.

He supposed she inspected the gun, judging by the way she turned it this way and that. The Colt revolver looked large and heavy in her small hands. Surely she'd never tried to use anything like it before. Maybe it had been a mistake to give it to her. But there were dangers in this wilderness. He had little use for women like her— uppity society sorts, which he could tell she was—but he still didn't feel comfortable leaving her alone.

He shook his head. What choice did he have? He didn't have enough jerky left to feed them both. While he could go without, she would need feeding. He needed to hunt, and hunting meant leaving her alone by the fire.

God, please don't let her shoot one of the horses or Bandit. Or me.

"I'll try not to be gone long, miss. Bandit, stay."

With that, he set off into the forest. With luck, he'd come upon a rabbit. Or maybe a rattlesnake. Snakes could be good eating if he cooked them right. He'd eaten worse things in his years in the West, although he doubted the pretty Englishwoman he'd pulled from the river could say the same.

———

A CHILL WENT through Amanda as Isaiah Coltrane disappeared into the trees. A chill that had nothing to do with the cool mountain air or even her wet clothing. The silence of the forest, broken only by the splash of the river near to the campsite, made her feel more alone than any other time in her life. Despite the sunlight spilling through the treetops, she felt the threat of nightfall. What if Mr. Coltrane didn't return? What if she was left alone? She felt lost. She had nothing to eat. Would she starve before someone found her? Or would a mountain lion or bear kill her first?

Do not be ridiculous. I shall be perfectly fine.

Leaving the revolver on the blanket, she clambered to her feet, then waited to see if the dizziness returned. But the world stayed upright and so did she. So far, so good. She stepped away from the fire and found a place of unbroken sunlight. Beneath his jacket, her damp clothes and wet hair clung to her skin. How she wished she could strip down to her undergarments and lay in the sun until everything was dry. Of course, she couldn't do that. She often strained against the rules of proper society, but she wasn't completely mad. Besides, there wasn't a great deal of warmth in the rays of the sun at this elevation.

Bandit came to sit next to her right leg, and Amanda leaned low to stroke the dog's head. "You take your charge seriously, don't you, boy? It's okay. I shall be fine."

But then she thought of William Overstreet, her brother's good friend and her host during the rest of her stay in America. He and Mrs. Adler, the Eden's Gate housekeeper, would give her so much grief over this escapade. And Roger. Oh, what Roger Bernhardt would have to say about her reckless behavior? All three would scold and lecture her. They would watch her like hawks from then on. She had promised them all that she would be safe with the touring group in the park. What could go wrong when she was with a large party led by professional guides? That's what she'd said to them—and she'd bent them to her will.

"I do not have to tell them this even happened," she said aloud. That made her feel better. No, she didn't have to tell them. She could keep the entire experience to herself.

Or could she? She sucked in a breath. Surely by now people would be searching for her. How many hours had she been gone from the tour group? When had someone first noticed her absence? Had it been minutes or hours? Whatever the length of time, it had been long enough for her to ride out of earshot.

But what did it matter? Whether others found her or Mr. Coltrane escorted her to the hotel on Yellowstone Lake or to Gardiner or back to the ranch, the result would be the same. She would have to tell the truth.

Shouldn't you always tell the truth?

She frowned. How inconvenient was that voice of her conscience.

Mr. Coltrane should know the truth, too.

A groan rumbled in her chest.

"The whole truth?" she wondered aloud.

Once again, she glanced around the campsite. The two horses grazed peacefully. Bandit watched her, alert but calm. The forest didn't seem as quiet now. She heard soft, scurrying sounds in the underbrush, and she imagined small animals like chipmunks and squirrels searching for nuts and berries. Insects buzzed. A twig cracked, perhaps a doe and fawn following a track through the tall trees. But none of those sounds caused her to feel threatened or endangered.

Amanda returned to the fire and added two more branches to the flames. Sparks flew into the air, then settled back into the fire. Sitting on the blanket, she removed the buckskin jacket. Next, she yanked off her wet riding boots and placed them as close to the fire as she dared.

Her brother would be so angry if he could see her now. Sebastian hadn't wanted to leave Amanda behind in America. It had taken all of her sisterly wiles to convince him that she would be fine. That remaining in America would give her time to mourn their father and recover from the loss. She'd told him she wouldn't be alone. Roger Bernhardt, his long-time friend, was remaining as well. And William—Sebastian's new brother-in-law—would keep a close eye on her while she stayed on his ranch. Again, what could go wrong?

A wry smile curved her mouth. "*I* could go wrong."

Even Amanda had to admit that her spontaneity had proven dangerous in the past. If not dangerous, then at least inconvenient for others. When an idea popped into her head, she tended to rush headlong into whatever it was without weighing ramifications.

"It isn't your finest attribute," Father had told her many a time.

Tears welled, a wave of grief rolling over her. Father's death had come so unexpectedly, even though he'd told them upon his arrival at the Overstreet ranch that he was dying, that his remaining time was short. He'd known he would never return to England, and still his death had taken her by surprise.

With the backs of her hands, she wiped away the tears tracking her cheeks. She sniffed, then took a deep breath, glad she could fill her lungs with air without coughing.

"I'll be fine." She focused her gaze on Bandit. "Your master seems frightfully trustworthy. You wouldn't obey him like this if he weren't trustworthy. Right?"

Even she knew that was nonsense, but it made her feel better to say it aloud.

Still, she believed she spoke the truth. Isaiah Coltrane had performed a selfless act. He'd risked his own safety in order to pull her from the river. The evil man who'd fired his gun at her could have returned and killed Isaiah while his attention was on her. Anxiety welled again. Those men could still return, she supposed.

She reached out and touched the revolver where it lay on the blanket, unsure if she was more afraid of those men returning or of picking up the gun again and attempting to use it.

Earlier that summer, she'd practiced shooting a Remington Derringer, although both she and Jocelyn had kept that a secret from Sebastian. The compact, double-barreled pistol had perfectly fit the size of Amanda's small hand. How she wished she had thought to get a pistol of her own before leaving on the excursion into the park.

Looking at Bandit, she said, "Or perhaps Mrs. Adler was right. I should have cancelled my trip. I should have remained at the ranch after Sebastian and Jocelyn left." She turned her gaze across the river to the forest and the mountains rising beyond them. "But I wanted to see all this. I wanted to experience it for myself. I believed being in this magnificent wilderness would heal my heart, make my grief seem more bearable." She drew a breath and let it out. "Besides, I'm so tired of others telling me what to do, what to think, what to feel."

Even her brother, almost from the moment he'd become the earl, had done that very thing. *Father was right, Amanda. You should be back at Hooke Manor. We need to find you a husband so you can marry and settle down.*

How could he say that to her? He'd come to America, at least partially, to escape their father's determined matchmaking. He'd met and fallen in love with

Jocelyn on Eden's Gate Ranch, and he'd defied their father to marry her. And now he wanted his younger sister to fall in line and marry a man of *his* choosing, not her own.

"I do not want that life. I want my own life. The one I choose."

Bandit edged closer and laid his head on Amanda's knee. She stroked the dog from head to haunches, drawing comfort from him.

"This could be my very last adventure before marriage," she whispered. And with that, the tears fell again.

Chapter Three

I t's me, miss."

Amanda's pulse quickened at the sound of Isaiah's voice coming from somewhere in the dense forest behind her. Dusk had painted the area in shades of gray, and she'd begun to dread the coming darkness even more than before. Not just the darkness but of being in it alone. She'd even wondered if she should saddle her horse and try to find her own way out of these lonely woods.

He appeared then, her rescuer, carrying two rabbits by their long ears.

She'd always thought rabbits adorable creatures and had never been fond of the idea of eating them. But at this precise moment, she was hungry enough to eat almost anything. She hadn't had a bite of food since breakfast, and she had eaten little of the greasy, partially cooked eggs and bacon prepared for the tour group that morning.

"Sorry it took so long." Isaiah lifted the rabbits a

little higher in the air. "And these won't be ready to eat for a while. Couple of hours, anyway."

"A couple of hours," she echoed softly. Her stomach grumbled.

His smile told her he'd heard the sound. "I've got a little jerky left. It'll tide you over." He laid the rabbits on the ground and went to his saddlebags. He returned with pieces of dried meat in one hand and a small cloth bag in the other.

"Thank you," she whispered as she took the jerky.

"That's the last, miss, but I've got some hardtack if you want it too."

"Mr. Coltrane, I cannot take all of your food."

He chuckled. "You're welcome to it. I've gone without food for more than one night. It won't kill me, especially knowing I've got some roast rabbit coming."

"You are a gentleman, sir."

He laughed again, louder this time.

Perhaps he was right to laugh. He didn't *look* like any gentleman she knew. Or at least the gentlemen she knew in England. While living on the ranch this summer, she'd learned that true gentlemen—men who were honest and caring and God-fearing—came packaged in all types of clothing.

She observed Isaiah as he set to work. He tied a rope between two nearby trees and hung the rabbits on it by their back legs. With a sharp knife, he made initial cuts around the first rabbit's legs and tail. At that point, she decided she didn't want to watch the entire skinning process and faced the fire again, thankful her clothes were nearly dry. With the coming of nightfall, the temperature had dropped even more. It was like that in these mountains, she'd learned. The days could be warm, but the nights were always cool. Sometimes cold. The touring company provided heated tents and cots at night, so she hadn't noticed it in the same way she did now.

"Miss?"

She startled at his voice a second time. "Yes?"

"You getting any memories back?"

This was her opportunity to tell the truth. She could give Isaiah her name. She could tell him where to take her to be reunited with the other tourists. It was reckless to continue with this charade. What if the tour guide sent word to William that she was missing? It wouldn't be right for her to cause him and the others to worry. He might set off with several of his cowboys to find her. That could cost William more than time. It could put his cattle operation at risk.

"I reckon you're in the park with one of those touring companies," Isaiah said, drawing her thoughts back to him. "You must've got yourself separated and lost while they were moving from one camping location to another."

She twisted on the blanket. Firelight danced across his features, as well as the rabbits, one of them now missing most of its skin. "What makes you say that?" she asked, even though he'd described the situation perfectly.

"Tourists are the only ones fool enough not to pay attention to their surroundings."

"I say, that is the second time you've called me a fool, sir."

"Can't help it if it's true, miss."

She was tired of being called miss, and she knew the way to stop it from continuing. She could tell him her name. She could inform him that she was Lady Amanda Whitcombe, currently staying on Eden's Gate Ranch in Idaho. She could tell him he was right. She had ridden away from the touring company with its wagons and horses and mules. With its tents and cots and food. With its men with rifles and guns to protect her and others. She'd ridden away on purpose and had become lost, just as he surmised. But now she was too annoyed to admit it. In fact, she didn't want to speak to him at all.

"In the morning," he said, "we'll head for the hotel on the lake. If we don't run into the touring company, the folks at the hotel will know what to do with you."

"What to *do* with me?" She stood. "I declare! Don't I have anything to say about where you take me?"

He stopped work on the rabbit. His expression told her nothing of what he thought of her questions. But after what seemed a long time, he said, "If you knew your name and how you got to be here, it might make a difference. As it is, I don't see I have any other option."

She turned her back to him, afraid he might see the truth in her eyes.

ISAIAH HID his amusement as he continued skinning the rabbits. He'd made her angry, and there was no denying he enjoyed knowing it. Women from the aristocracy—and there was no way this young woman with her speech, bearing, and beauty wasn't from the titled class of England—could get under his skin quicker than a coiled rattler could strike. He'd been around a fair share of wealthy, privileged women when he lived in Washington D.C., and he hadn't been sorry to leave them behind.

In truth, he couldn't remember anything about his old life that he missed, except for his parents. And they'd both passed away years ago, even before he decided to follow the pathways of the mountain men he admired. He'd been born too late for many of the things he'd hoped to experience for himself. The massive herds of buffalo were gone. The Indian tribes lived on reservations instead of roaming freely over the mountains and valleys they'd called home for generations. Territories had become states, states with towns and cities popping up from border to border. Railroads stretched from sea to sea, in the north and in the south, allowing Americans to travel with an ease never imagined.

Still, there was much of this amazing country that remained wild and free, and Isaiah had found his own small patch of it to call home. He was content to live alone in his cabin north of Yellowstone Park. He could provide his own food. He had books to read, and he had journals to write in. He liked his own thoughts and his own company. In addition, he enjoyed the challenge of tracking poachers and bringing them to justice. It gave him satisfaction to protect big game in the park. It didn't bother him to not see another human being for weeks or even months at a time in the deep of winter. And when he had one of his rare guests, they always had grand stories to tell, stories Isaiah often recorded in his journals.

His gaze returned to the unnamed woman by the fire. The one wearing his coat. Did she remember more than she was willing to say? There was a lump on her head. No denying it. But was it—and perhaps the shock of the cold water—enough to steal her memory all these hours later? Maybe so, but his skepticism remained. There was something about her . . .

As if feeling his gaze upon her, she faced him once again. "Mr. Coltrane?"

"Yes." He returned to his work with the rabbits.

"You must be right. I must have been with a tour group and become separated from them. But I . . . But perhaps there was a good reason I rode off by myself."

He glanced up. "And what good reason could that be?" He took a step toward her. "Look, I know most of the people who run the touring companies in the park. They're good people. They take care of their guests. Got to if they want to stay in business. There'd be no reason that makes sense for a woman like yourself to ride away from them on purpose."

She worried her lower lip between her teeth, and her eyes narrowed, perhaps considering what to say next.

Again, he wondered if she knew more than she let on. And if she was lying to him, why wasn't he angry because of it? She'd cost him days and money. He probably wouldn't even catch those poachers this time around. Yet he found himself intrigued instead of irritated.

With a huff that sounded suspiciously like frustration, she turned again and settled on the blanket by the fire.

"You might want to get some sleep, miss. There's another blanket there by my saddle." He set to work with the knife. "We can dine on these rabbits for breakfast."

Chapter Four

A manda opened her eyes to a sky announcing dawn in shades of pink and orange. The fire blazed hot, telling her she wasn't the first to awaken. Mixed with the crisp morning air was the scent of cooked meat, and her stomach rumbled in response.

"Morning." Isaiah's deep, masculine voice did something quite different to her stomach.

Sitting up, she looked around and found him sitting on a log, a slice of roasted rabbit in his right hand. "Have you been awake long?"

"Long enough."

She suspected that meant he hadn't slept most of the night. Perhaps he hadn't slept at all. Between skinning rabbits by firelight, cooking the meat, keeping the fire hot, watching the horses, and making sure she was protected, when would he have slept? She rose to her feet, noticing all the places that ached from a night on the hard, lumpy ground. After putting on her boots— only a slight dampness remained—she straightened and turned in a slow circle while looking for a place of privacy to take care of her most pressing need.

"Take Bandit with you," Isaiah said. "He'll keep you safe."

Heat rose up her neck and into her cheeks. Keeping her eyes averted from Isaiah, she said, "Bandit, come." The dog moved to her side.

How mortifying, that he should understand so quickly where she was going, what she was doing. And yet, she hadn't felt embarrassed at such times during her time with the touring company. Of course, they had permanent camps with cots and mattresses and tents. Not to mention basic facilities to accommodate their female guests.

Amanda wasn't a hot house flower. The past few months on the Overstreet ranch had been proof of that. She'd helped round up cattle, for pity sake, and had even ridden with a few of the ranch hands as they'd searched for rustlers. Yes, she'd been raised in luxury, but she was not afraid to get her hands dirty. She'd known it would be true even before she arrived at Eden's Gate.

When she returned from the seclusion of the forest, she found both horses saddled and bridled. Isaiah had rolled up the blankets and begun to put other items into his saddlebags.

"There's some of the roast meat there." He motioned to a tin plate on a rock next to the fire.

"Thank you." Taking the plate with her, she went to the log and sat where he'd sat not long before.

"We'll head south from here," he told her. "With this

early of a start, we should have you to the hotel by supper time."

"Mr. Coltrane . . . I . . ." She took a deep breath and stiffened her spine. "Would you . . . could I hire you to take me . . . home?"

He stopped and met her gaze across the campsite. "You've remembered something?"

She nodded.

"Including your name?"

She nodded again.

"Then I suppose you ought to tell me."

She drew another breath. "Amanda. Amanda Whitcombe."

"From?"

"My home is in Lincolnshire."

"In England."

"Yes."

"Should I address you as *Lady* Amanda?"

Was he mocking her? She lifted her chin. "If you wish. It is the proper form of address, although few Americans bother with it."

He smiled, and her breath caught in response.

"Thought as much. Your kind like to visit Yellowstone. Nothing like it in good old England, is there?"

"My *kind*?" That breathless feeling vanished, replaced by the heat of displeasure. "Perhaps not, but there are plenty other things to admire and love in England. Our family estate is beautiful. The land is fertile and the weather is mild. We have—"

"Sorry." He held up both hands. "Sorry. I didn't mean to insult your homeland."

"Of course you did." She stood and carried the plate and cup to the river's edge. Squatting on the bank, she rinsed the items clean, then rose and returned them to Isaiah. "Thank you." Her tone was as glacial as the water.

He cleared his throat. "You mentioned wanting to hire me to take you somewhere other than Yellowstone Lake."

"Yes. I would like to go back to the ranch where I am staying through the winter. It's outside the park in Idaho."

"In Idaho?" He cocked an eyebrow at her. "You're living there, on a ranch?"

She ignored the questions. "But we must go to the hotel on the lake first. That mare is the property of the touring company, and my travel bag is in one of their wagons. And I don't want anyone sending out a search party for me or sending word that I am missing. So I believe we need to go to the lake first. I simply do not want to remain with the touring company afterward."

He frowned. "Miss Whitcombe, did something happen that I should know about? Did one of their men do something that—"

"No!" Heat rose up her neck again. "No, nothing like that."

The truth was, it was difficult to explain her reasons for wanting to go back to Eden's Gate. She'd loved seeing the wild beauty of the park. The animals. The waterfalls. The rivers and streams. She knew she hadn't seen more than a fraction of the more than twenty million acres that made up Yellowstone, but suddenly she wanted to be back with her friends more than anything else. And for some reason she could not fathom, she hoped Isaiah Coltrane would be the man who took her there.

———

ISAIAH WATCHED several different emotions cross Amanda's pretty face. He couldn't name them all. Perhaps anger and frustration. Perhaps determination. But definitely sadness and grief. And the grief came with tears.

"I'm sorry," she whispered as she turned away from him.

The pain in her voice caught at his heart. "Miss Whitcombe."

"I'm all right. It . . . it's nothing."

True, women could cry over nothing. He'd seen it done. A few he'd known could cry on cue, like a performer on stage. But that wasn't what had happened to Amanda Whitcombe. He was sure of it. Her tears were real, and so was whatever memory had caused the heartbreak.

"Miss Whitcombe," he tried again. "You needn't worry. I'll see you to wherever you want to go. I'll take you to the ranch in Idaho. You won't come to any harm as long as you're with me."

"Oh, sir." From somewhere on her person she retrieved a handkerchief, and she used it to dab at her eyes. "I'm not crying to . . . to convince you to take me to the ranch. I want to go back there. Very much. But I'm crying because . . . because of my father."

Confusion made Isaiah blink. "Your father?"

"Yes, he . . . he died."

"When?" Alarm shot through him. "On this trip?"

She shook her head. "No. No, but not long ago. Only a few weeks. I . . . I never should have come to the park. They told me I shouldn't. My family. My friends. They told me I should cancel my reservation with the touring company." The words tumbled out of her, one on top of the other like rushing water from a burst dam. "But you see, my visit to Yellowstone was already cancelled once before. I became ill in the summer, and so I wasn't able to come to the park as planned. I didn't want to cancel a second time. Summer is almost over. There will not be another opportunity before I return to England. William says winter arrives early in these mountains, and I wouldn't even be able to come into the park once the snow falls. And that could be soon, I understand."

William? Who was William?

"I so wanted to see all this amazing land. The rivers and waterfalls. The buffalo. Old Faithful. Everything I've read and heard about. But I . . . I suppose I wasn't ready to be away from my family yet. Sebastian and Jocelyn are gone now, of course. He had to return to take charge of Hooke Manor." Tears welled in her eyes once more. "But the ranch feels like home to me and the people on it are my friends. Dear friends. It would be better for me to be with them. I realize that now." She sniffed. "Oh, how I wish I was with them. If you really could take me home . . ." She stopped speaking as quickly as she'd begun, and silence fell over the campsite.

Isaiah was used to quiet. Weeks and even months of it at a time when the only voice he heard was his own when he spoke to his dog. But this silence left him feeling uncertain, unsure what to do with it.

He watched as she dried her eyes once more. Then she straightened her shoulders and lifted her head. Even as small as she was, he saw the determined strength of her character. He drew in a breath, as if he too needed to call up his courage. He'd made her a promise to take her wherever she wished to go. He'd promised to escort her to Idaho. It was a promise rashly made, without doubt, but he'd made it. "What's the name of the place where I'm to take you, miss?"

"Eden's Gate."

He'd heard of the ranch. A large spread in Idaho, a good two days ride from his place outside Gardiner, Montana. "All right then. We'll go to the lake today. Catch up with your tour group. If they've got men out searching for you—and I don't doubt that they do— hopefully we'll run into them on the way. We'll get your belongings and make certain the folks at Eden's Gate know you're all right, if they've been alerted you were missing. We'll have to buy you a horse, too." He bumped the brim of his hat, knocking it back from his forehead. "But I need to ask. Are you sure about this? We're talking a number of days travel by horseback and sleeping on the ground. You could arrange to take the stage from the lake up to Gardiner, then hire a private coach to take you down to the ranch. Might have to wait a few extra days for the stage, but the hotel would probably have room for you."

Steel seemed to enter her gaze. "I am certain this is what I want, Mr. Coltrane. I do not relish the notion of that journey in a stagecoach. I would much rather be in the saddle. Horseback is far more comfortable. And I will not complain or be a burden to you. I promise you that."

Isaiah believed her, although he wasn't sure why. She might be wealthy and from the British titled class. She might be used to a life of ease and comfort. But she didn't put on airs as he'd expected. At least not most of the time. She didn't expect him to wait on her or cater to her. She wasn't afraid to do what was necessary. That had been clear enough, even before her memory returned. Perhaps he wouldn't regret his rash promise to deliver her to the ranch in Idaho.

"Then we'd best get started," he said, turning toward the horses, attempting to put resolve in his voice.

Chapter Five

W*hy do I trust him?*

Amanda watched the man in front of her as they traversed a narrow trail through the forest. He didn't seem to be in any hurry to catch up with the touring company wagons, although he'd stated that was his intent. His buckskin flicked his tail, and Bandit darted off through the trees, perhaps chasing a squirrel or chipmunk, then bounded back again. The dog didn't bark, which surprised her, and he constantly looked toward his master, as if awaiting a command.

Perhaps Bandit was the reason she trusted Isaiah Coltrane. That dog was devoted to the man leading them through the forest, and Amanda couldn't help but think it spoke to Isaiah's good character. Her brothers would scoff at her reasoning, but she believed it anyway.

Some time in late morning, the forest gave way to an expanse of meadow. A doe and two fawns grazed in the long grasses opposite them, but they darted into the trees once they spotted the horses and riders.

Isaiah reined in. "Let's get a stretch of the legs while we're here. After that we're going to ride faster. Up ahead's the road the touring companies use to transport their guests to the lake." He pointed, perhaps to reassure her.

After dismounting—with Bandit as her protector once again—Amanda found a secluded place to take care of private matters. When she returned, she found Isaiah holding the reins to both horses. He passed the mare's reins to her.

"We'll walk a bit," he said, stepping out.

She quickly fell in beside him. Since leaving camp, they'd journeyed in silence, mostly because she'd had to follow behind him, making conversation difficult. That was no longer true, and she was ready to learn more about the man she'd trusted with her fate over the next few days.

"Mr. Coltrane," she began, "yesterday you said you were tracking poachers and that perhaps they were the men who shot at me. Is that . . . catching poachers . . . what you do?"

"For the past several summers. The park hires a few game scouts every year to help keep down the killing of wildlife. Big game. Not animals like the rabbits I shot last night."

"Do you live in the park?"

"No. I've got a cabin of my own up near Gardiner."

"Gardiner. That's where the tour started from. Will we return there before heading down into Idaho? You said that's the route the stagecoach takes."

"No. We'll take an old trail through the mountains

west of us. Wagons can't use it but we can make it on horseback. You'll get to see more of the park you haven't seen on your tour, and it will get you home sooner."

She liked the sound of his plans. She had no need to see Gardiner again. "Have you lived in Montana all your life?"

"No." He smiled without glancing her way. "Less than six years now."

"Where are you from?"

"Back east. I grew up near Washington, D.C. Studied law at Georgetown University. That was my father's wish for me. To be a lawyer."

Amanda stumbled over a rough patch of ground— and was thankful for it. It kept her from responding to him in surprise. He didn't look or sound like a man who'd studied the law at a university. He looked like the mountain men of her imagination or even the cowboys who worked William's cattle ranch. She couldn't picture Isaiah in tailcoat and dress trousers, seated in the House of Lords, the way her brother soon would be, or clad in a three-piece suit, standing before a judge in a court of law in America's capital city.

Although Isaiah had steadied her with his right hand on her elbow, he kept his eyes focused ahead, ever watchful. And as if there'd been no pause in the conversation, he continued. "After my father died, I made the decision to leave the east. It was long my dream to do so, and there seemed no reason not to after his passing."

"And your mother?"

"She died when I was ten."

"How frightfully sad." Amanda drew a breath. "I was five when my mother died. It left a large hole in my life."

"But you were close to your father." The way he said it, she wasn't sure if his words were a statement or question.

"I should think so. Very close. He had a more difficult relationship with Sebastian, my brother and his heir. But Father and I—" She broke off when a lump formed in her throat.

"I'm guessing your father danced to your pretty tune, Miss Whitcombe."

She shook her head, still unable to answer.

At last he looked her way. The smile he'd worn faded, and he stopped walking, causing her to do the same. "I'm sorry. I didn't mean that unkindly."

"I know." She forced the smallest of smiles, memories of her father at Hooke Manor floating through her mind. "And to be honest, he did give me my way quite often. Perhaps more often than not."

"Spoiled you, did he?"

"Perhaps a little." Her smile was more heartfelt now.

"I don't blame him. I'd probably spoil you too."

ISAIAH COULDN'T BELIEVE he'd said that. And from the look in her wide eyes, Lady Amanda Whitcombe couldn't believe he'd said it either. And then she laughed, the sound airy and light, floating upward like steam rising from one of the hot springs scattered throughout the park.

He cleared his throat. "We'd best mount up and get to riding."

"Rather!" She sounded as if she were stifling more laughter.

Isaiah swung into the saddle and urged Buck into a swift walk. As soon as he knew Amanda followed close behind, he nudged the gelding into a trot and finally into a canter. They continued that way—Isaiah leading, Amanda following—for several miles before he slowed his mount to a walk and finally brought him to a halt.

Bandit moved out in front of Buck and sat with his tongue lolling out one side of his mouth. But after a short while, the dog rose to all fours again, his gaze locked on a forested area up ahead. Isaiah took heed, his hand moving to the butt of the rifle.

"What is it?" Amanda asked.

"Not sure." Then he heard it. Voices. Men's voices calling out a name. Calling out *her* name. He glanced over his shoulder. "It's the search team looking for you." Straightening in the saddle, he cupped his mouth with one hand and shouted, "Up ahead."

Moments later, three riders came out of the trees. As they drew closer, Isaiah recognized the man in the lead. Jed Dunlap, one of the guides of the touring company. In his fifties, his face was leathered from years in the elements.

"Isaiah Coltrane," Jed called. "Is that you?"

"It's me. And I believe I've found what you're

looking for." He glanced over his shoulder a second time.

Amanda nudged the mare forward until she was beside Isaiah and Buck.

"Miss Whitcombe." Surprise and relief washed over Jed's grizzled face. "We feared we'd lost you for good. Wasn't sure how long you'd been missing. Didn't realize 'til we stopped for the noon meal yesterday that you weren't with us."

"I am frightfully sorry, Mr. Dunlap. I never meant to cause any trouble. I got turned around so quickly in the forest and couldn't find my way back."

Jed frowned. "Where'd you find her, Coltrane?"

Isaiah gave a quick recap of the previous day, adding, "I figured we'd run into you, the good Lord willing, if we got an early start this morning."

"Sorry you lost out on catching those poachers."

"Me too." He glanced at Amanda. "But I'm thankful nothing worse happened."

"Well, we'll be right glad to take her off your hands."

"Mr. Dunlap," Amanda said quickly, "I've decided not to rejoin the tour."

"Miss?"

"I only wanted to make sure no one alerted my friends at Eden's Gate and to collect my things. Then I'm returning to Idaho."

"Do you plan to take a rest at the Yellowstone Lake House?"

"Only for a night or two. I'm eager to go home."

Jed removed his hat and scratched his head with his

little finger. "You unhappy with the tour, Miss Whitcombe? 'Cause we'd sure hate to hear that. Most of our guests have a right good time. Don't know what we could've done different to make sure you didn't get lost the way you—"

"It wasn't anyone's fault but my own that I became separated and lost," she interrupted quickly. "I assure you of that."

The guide continued as if she hadn't spoken. "You'll have to make arrangements to get back to Gardiner. Don't know how long that'll take you or what you might have to pay."

"Mr. Dunlap, please. Do not worry about any of it. I have made my own arrangements. And I have only good things to say about your touring company. My reasons for leaving have nothing to do with dissatisfaction."

The older man shook his head, looking confused.

Isaiah understood. Amanda Whitcombe had left him feeling confused more than once, and he'd only met her yesterday. "Jed, don't worry. I mean to see Miss Whitcombe safely back to her home in Idaho."

"You?"

Isaiah shrugged.

"Well, I reckon she'll be safe, long as she's with you." The guide turned his horse south. "Don't make sense to me, but there's plenty in life that don't."

Chapter Six

The Yellowstone Lake House was far grander and more elegant than Amanda expected. Located on the north shore of the lake, the hotel offered its wealthy guests—most of them arriving by stagecoach—stunning views of the water and the surrounding mountains and wilderness.

Amanda was only too glad that night to eat a splendid dinner in her spacious bedroom before taking a bath and sinking into the nice, soft bed. Roughing it was great fun, to be sure, but there was something to be said for the finer amenities in life.

As she drifted off to sleep, she wondered if Isaiah's accommodations were as nice as her own. When she opened her eyes more than eight hours later, the same thought lingered in her consciousness. But this time the question disturbed her. She hadn't asked Isaiah if he had the finances to stay in the hotel. And if he hadn't stayed in the hotel, where had he stayed?

Shame warmed her cheeks as she sat up in the bed.

How thoughtless she was! He'd saved her from the river. He'd fed her from his own supplies. He'd brought her safely to this wonderful hotel. He'd been polite and gentlemanly. He'd made her feel safe and secure. And she'd given no thought to what he would do or where he would stay until they departed for Eden's Gate.

Amanda reclined once more, several pillows at her back. Perhaps she worried needlessly. She hoped that was the case. While she didn't imagine Isaiah earned a great deal of money catching poachers in the national park, he didn't appear to need or require or even want someone like her to see to his needs. He was the sort of man who took care of himself. A man as rugged as the mountains where he made his home.

Imagine. Years ago, Isaiah left what she assumed had been a comfortable living back in the east. He'd abandoned a university education and his father's plans that he become a lawyer. He'd left behind everything he'd known and come to the Rocky Mountains. And he'd done it all alone. Was his cabin near Gardiner secluded or did he have neighbors? How did he spend his winters? Did he hunt and trap in addition to tracking poachers?

Would I have that kind of courage, given the choice?

The question swirled in her mind for a long while before she released a sound of annoyance. What would it matter if she had the same kind of courage as Isaiah? She wouldn't be given the choice because she wasn't a man. It wasn't fair but it was true.

With a huff, she tossed aside the blankets and rose to meet the day.

Half an hour later, washed and dressed, she made her way to the registration desk.

"May I help you, miss?" the clerk behind the desk asked.

"Indeed. I was wondering. Did a Mr. Coltrane stay in the hotel last night?"

The young man looked at her, perhaps wondering what her business was with a Mr. Coltrane. Did he think her reasons were disreputable? But after a while, he glanced down at the large book and scanned the signatures on the open pages. "No, miss. He is not registered at the hotel."

"Thank you." She lifted her chin as she turned toward the dining room.

He wasn't a guest of the hotel. So where was he? When would she see him again? They'd made no specific plans after they'd reached the lake. He'd left her at the registration desk, telling her that he needed to take care of the horses and would see her in the morning. But what time this morning? And where?

As if summoned by her thoughts, she saw him rise at a table at the far end of the expansive dining room. Tall and broad-shouldered, there was no mistaking him, even from a distance.

The maître d' approached. "Are you dining alone, miss?"

"No." She smiled, her gaze lingering on Isaiah. "I am with that gentleman."

"Very well. Please follow Jason." He pointed to another, younger man in a white jacket.

Jason, the waiter, led the way through tables where

couples, families, and groups ate their breakfasts. Beyond the windows, the rays of a golden sun reflected off the surface of the water. In the distance, mountains rose in majestic display. But it was Isaiah himself who held her attention. Although his clothes looked to be the same, they appeared cleaner than the last time she'd seen him in them. So did the man himself. He'd obviously bathed and washed his hair, and his jaw was freshly shaved.

"Good morning, Miss Whitcombe," he said as she and the waiter approached.

"Good morning, Mr. Coltrane." Odd, the jittery feeling in her stomach. "I wondered when we would meet today." Jason held out a chair for her, and she settled on it.

"Did you sleep well?" Isaiah asked. "And how's that bump on your head? Giving you any pain?"

"I slept exceedingly well. Thank you. And my head is tender but better." She touched the lump, checking the truth of her answer. "How did you sleep, sir?"

A smile tugged at the corners of his mouth. "Well enough."

"But not in one of the hotel beds."

"No, Miss Whitcombe. Not in one of their beds."

"I knew it." She shook her head. "I was thoughtless not to offer you accommodation. Do forgive me, won't you? You are, after all, now in my employ."

His smile broadened. "I am in your employ, miss, but I don't expect or require a hotel room. Bandit and I are used to sleeping under the stars. We like it better that way."

"I have enjoyed nights under the stars too." She placed the cloth napkin on her lap, needing something to do rather than continue to stare at him. "But I confess it was rather nice to be in a bed last night, and I should have made sure you enjoyed the same."

"Good you got to enjoy it, because we'll be sleeping on the ground again soon enough." He looked at the waiter who stood nearby. "Perhaps you should tell him what you want for breakfast. I've already ordered mine."

Amanda glanced at the menu. As soon as Jason had her order and walked away, she said, "Soon enough? What does that mean?"

Isaiah sipped coffee from a delicate china cup. "If you're up to it, I wouldn't mind getting started today. I think we can be ready to go right after lunch."

"I'm up to it."

"I've found a horse for you. Belongs to a friend of mine so we won't have to buy one for you."

"But I said I would buy one. I have the funds."

"No need. Paddy's in no hurry to get the horse back, and I know this little gelding. Good mountain horse." He took another sip of coffee, the cup looking ridiculously small in his big hand. "I've got us a pack mule too. We won't be traveling as light as I'm used to doing. There won't be time for hunting game either, so we have to carry what we'll need. We want to get you home without delay."

Did he mean he was eager to be rid of her? That jittery sensation in her stomach turned to lead.

Isaiah noticed the change that came over Amanda. She didn't seem to want to look at him, and she answered his remaining questions and comments with a terse word or two. Very unlike her. He found he missed her usual wordiness. Which came as a surprise.

The silence continued after their food arrived. Since there was no reason to linger over breakfast, he cleaned his plate in a hurry, then pushed it back from the edge of the table. "I'd better get to it," he said, preparing to rise.

"Where shall I meet you when it is time to leave?"

"Right out front. I'll have the horses and pack mule there, ready to go. Shall we say one o'clock? That should give me time to buy the rest of our supplies and get back here."

"I should come with you. I need to pay for the supplies."

"You can repay me, Miss Whitcombe. No need for me to drag you around while I buy supplies and see to the horses and pack mule."

"Are you saying I would be in your way?"

He'd seen that spark in her eyes before, heard that tinge of vexation in her voice. And he couldn't help it. He grinned. Even when she irritated him, there was something about her that made him want to smile. He couldn't explain why. He'd never known the like.

Realizing his grin had only served to increase her annoyance with him, he schooled his features and answered, "No, I'm not saying that, Miss Whitcombe. I just don't think it's necessary. I can do this faster on my own. I know what we need and where things are and the people I can depend on to supply them."

His answer seemed to mollify her, at least somewhat, and she nodded. "All right. I will meet you at one o'clock in front of the hotel."

He settled his hat on his head.

"Mr. Coltrane, I forgot to ask. How long will it take us to reach Eden's Gate?"

"If we don't run into any trouble, it's possible it could be done in a bit over three and a half days. I'm guessing it'll take us four and a half."

"Three and a half should do it." She nodded again, then stood before he could pull out her chair.

He motioned for her to precede him through the dining room, still busy at this hour. But it wouldn't be long before many of the tourists were out enjoying nature, some more overtly than others. At least Amanda Whitcombe was dressed for the experience. Some society women came to the park wearing bustles and corsets so tight it cut off air supply.

"I am not a fool, Mr. Coltrane."

No, he'd learned as much over the past couple of days. She might come from the British aristocracy, she might even have made some foolish choices that caused her to be shot at and thrown into a river, but she was not a fool. That he was willing to admit. Even more surprising, he looked forward to the coming days in her company.

Maybe I'm *the fool.*

He parted from Amanda in the lobby and set about

completing preparations for their journey. He retrieved the horses and mule from the corral where he'd left them, guarded by Bandit. After saddling and bridling the horses, he led the three animals to the general store. Before long, he'd purchased the additional items they would need for the journey. Hardtack, jerky, salt pork, beans, coffee, salt, sugar. A skillet for cooking. Plenty of matches. Another tin cup, plate, and eating utensils. An extra canteen. Some grain for the horses and mules, along with two nosebags. Several more blankets and a couple of oilcloths. A bar of soap and a couple small towels. Another pair of hobbles, this one for the mule, and more ammunition for his revolver and rifle.

Loading all of the supplies onto the pack saddle and into saddlebags didn't take long. Many times, he'd prepared for trips similar to this one—minus the beautiful young woman who would accompany him, of course—and he knew how to spread the weight over horses and mule and how to give himself easy access to what he would need most frequently.

As Isaiah packed the final item, Paddy Muldoon approached. The Irishman, his good friend, stopped beside the brown and white pinto and gave the horse a pat on the neck. "Headin' out soon?"

Isaiah nodded as he tightened the cinch on the pack saddle, earning a complaint from the mule.

"Takin' the Mary Mountain Trail?"

"That's my plan."

Paddy looked at the sky. "If a storm comes, and I'm thinkin' it could, it'll bring snow with it up in the passes."

If there was any man who could guess the weather,

Paddy Muldoon was that man. Isaiah had made his acquaintance soon after setting foot in Montana. Despite their age differences—Paddy being in his sixties and Isaiah in his twenties—they'd formed a close friendship.

"We should be fine," Isaiah answered.

"This girl you're taking. Is she ready for that kind of trip? You might be better off sending her by stagecoach to Gardiner. I coulda seen her there if you wanted."

"You're right. I might be better off that way. But she wasn't keen on riding the stage, and I made her a promise. Gotta keep it now."

"You sweet on her?"

Isaiah straightened away from the mule. "Am I *what*?"

"You heard me."

"I only met her two days ago."

"So you told me. But sometimes that's all the time it takes. Besides, this just ain't like you, Isaiah."

He grunted a response before turning back to the animals. He tied the mule's lead rope to Buck's saddle horn, then took the reins of both horses in his hand. As he started to lead them away, he said, "I should be back in Gardiner in about a week. If there's a delay in my return, I'll send you word."

"You'd better let me know," Paddy called after him. "I don't want to be searching these mountains for you. I'm gettin' too old for such nonsense."

Walking toward the hotel, he wondered if his friend was right. He could have kept his promise to Amanda another way. He could have seen that she got back to

Eden's Gate by entrusting her to others. But then he remembered the look in her eyes as she'd told him about her father's passing. He remembered the brokenhearted expression she'd worn and how desperately she'd wanted to be home. He'd seen and understood the grief because he'd known it himself, and he'd had no choice but to promise her a swift return to those who could comfort her.

"If anything goes wrong," he said to Bandit, trotting beside him, "it'll be all my own fault."

Chapter Seven

I saiah set a steady pace, sometimes walking the horses, occasionally trotting. He wanted to cover at least ten miles before they made camp for the night. For today and a good portion of the next, they would follow the main road, the one that stagecoaches used to and from Gardiner. He told Amanda they might even come across some of the wagons used by the touring companies. But at the end of August, those were fewer and farther between than in July.

Amanda seemed content to enjoy the views of the Yellowstone River that peeked through the trees on their right. Her quiet worried him a little, but whenever he inquired if she was all right, she answered that she was.

Several times during that afternoon—the soft warmth of the sun allowing them to remove their jackets —they witnessed long Vs of geese flying south and heard them honking to one another, even from high in the sky. An immense elk herd grazed in a meadow on their left as shadows began to lengthen. A word to Bandit kept the dog from instigating a game of chase.

There was still more than an hour of daylight remaining when he found a good campsite. With practiced ease, he removed supplies and saddles from the horses and mule, fed them some grain, then hobbled and turned them loose to graze. The animals cared for, he turned his attention to making a fire and preparing their evening meal.

As had become a habit already, Amanda had gone into the trees, seeking privacy, his dog at her side. When she returned, he had beans heating in a tin pot and salt pork sizzling in the frying pan.

"Mind keeping an eye on the food?" he asked her. "I'll go fill the canteens and wash the dust off."

She nodded in agreement, but his intention was to return quickly. He wasn't convinced she wouldn't burn herself or their dinner if he wasn't back in time.

A short while later, kneeling beside the river, he splashed his face with the frigid water and scrubbed the back of his neck with one hand. Next he held the canteens, one at a time, under the river's surface, filling them to the brim. When he returned to the campsite, he discovered the pot of beans had been moved from the fire, and the salt pork had been turned onto the opposite side, cooking to perfection. Amanda watched his approach, and something in her stance told him she knew he'd feared failure on her part.

He managed to swallow a smile before giving her an abrupt nod of his head.

It wasn't long before they sat opposite each other

across the fire, hot food on their plates, cold water in their canteens to wash it down. At first the only sounds heard were the crackling of the fire, the cool breeze in the pines, and the scratch of utensils on tin plates. But eventually, Amanda broke the silence that had stretched between them, and Isaiah was glad of it.

"My father never understood my fascination with the American West. He thought it extraordinary foolishness. But I was captivated by Buffalo Bill and his Wild West show when they performed for the queen." She looked upward at a sky that had turned from blue to pewter. "It really is everything I dreamed it would be. Frightfully exciting, all of it. Everything and more." When she lowered her gaze again, there were tears in her eyes. "Father would be horrified if he could see me now."

"Why?"

"I was meant to be a proper lady like my mother." She pushed loose strands of hair back from her face, forcing a smile. "You should have seen the way Father looked at me the first time he saw me in a split skirt and riding astride." She laughed but it held little humor.

"Your clothes are sensible, given what we're doing." He could have said she looked every inch a lady, no matter what she wore. "And riding astride is safer, especially here in these mountains," As Isaiah spoke, Paddy's voice whispered in his memory, *"You sweet on her?"*

Sweet on Amanda? No. But he was so unused to female company that he couldn't help taking notice of most everything about her. The way her long, dark hair hung in a thick braid over one shoulder. The way her skirt fell from her narrow waist and rounded hips, the length of it hitting a few inches below the tops of her riding boots. The way she watched him with those eyes of hers. Brown eyes that reminded him of the bottom of a forest pond, a pond that held secrets in its depths. Eyes that at the moment had turned misty again. Probably because her thoughts had turned to her father and his passing.

"So tell me," he said, hoping to disrupt her thoughts, "how long have you been in America?"

"We arrived in Idaho in May."

"We?"

"My brother Sebastian and his friend Roger Bernhardt and I. We were on the ranch a couple of months before Father joined us unexpectedly."

Isaiah had hoped to make her forget her father for a while, but his efforts hadn't worked.

Amanda blinked, her gaze locked on the dancing fire between them. "He was quite ill when he arrived, but he rallied and was able to see my brother married to Jocelyn Overstreet. And he seemed . . . content when he passed. More at peace, I think, than he'd been in a long while." She brushed her cheeks with her fingertips. "I'm sorry. I don't mean to cry. I'm not usually prone to tears."

"You needn't apologize, Miss Whitcombe. Not to me."

"I wasn't weepy when I began my excursion into the park. I thought I was past that point. I knew I would always miss my father, but . . ." Her voice drifted into silence.

"Grief takes most of us by surprise, even when we've expected the loss. And it takes longer to get over than most folks want." He thought of the deaths of his parents. As a boy, he'd cried over his mother. He hadn't completely understood what had happened or why she was gone, never to return. By the time his father passed, he'd learned not to show his emotions in the same way. His self-control hadn't lessened the loss he'd felt on the inside, but it had hidden it from others.

Softly, Amanda said, "Someone told me time heals all wounds. Do you suppose that is true, Mr. Coltrane?"

"Most wounds, I'd say. But not all. The pain lessens. The wound remains. Or at least an awful scar."

She sniffed, then sat straighter on the log that served as a stool. "A great deal of responsibility has fallen onto Sebastian's shoulders. He knew it would happen one day, of course. He knew he would be the next earl. But Father seemed so hale and hearty. When we left England we didn't even know he was ill. He'd kept his suspicions from us for I don't know how long." She took a breath, her shoulders rising and falling. "My brother meant to spend a full year in America, and I thought he might remain longer even after Father died. But he knew he would be needed back in England."

"But you chose to stay."

"It wasn't easy to convince him to allow it." She released a soft laugh. "He wanted to forbid me to remain behind. But he would have been forced to contradict all the things he said to Father last spring when we planned this trip. And Jocelyn, my new sister-in-law, was on my side. Sebastian couldn't deny her even though he wanted to deny me."

Isaiah remembered how quickly he'd promised to escort Amanda to Eden's Gate Ranch and felt a kinship with her brother. Perhaps it wasn't the strength of an argument or the persuasion of her sister-in-law. Perhaps Amanda's tears had won over Sebastian, the same way they'd won over Isaiah.

He gave his head a slight shake, glad that her tears were gone for now. She was more her talkative self, and he wanted to keep it that way. Apparently talkative and weepy didn't go together. "Tell me how you came to stay at Eden's Gate."

"William Overstreet, the owner of the ranch, was sent to school in England as a boy. He and Sebastian became friends there and remained so after William returned to America. William issued a number of invitations for my brother to come visit him, and eventually Sebastian accepted. Roger and I were allowed to join him." She smiled. "I think of William as another brother."

Her smile—brief though it was—seemed to light up their campsite even more than the fire did.

She continued, "I have a friend who married an American. A man who was in the Wild West show that came to England for the Jubilee. I was able to visit their ranch in Washington earlier this summer, and I bought one of their Palouse horses. A three-year-old mare. She's beautiful. I plan to take her back to England and breed her to one of the Whitcombe studs."

Isaiah's attention sharpened. "Your family raises horses?"

"Indeed. We have wonderful stables at Hooke Manor. My half-brother, Adam, manages it. And he believes we have a good chance of winning the Grand National in another year or two."

"The Grand National. Impressive." Odd. He'd almost forgotten Amanda Whitcombe was a member of the aristocracy, even after she'd brought up her brother's responsibilities as the new earl. It took mentioning the Whitcombe stables and the possibility of winning the Grand National to remind him that she was a *Lady* with a capital *L*.

"Ebony, my Palouse mare, has great potential."

"Do you mean to race her?"

"Oh, no. She's for pleasure riding only. But I can't wait to show her off to my friends. We don't have horses colored like her in England. You'll see for yourself when we get to the ranch."

As he nodded, he realized the sun had set as they ate and talked. Darkness had overtaken the forest surrounding them and the night had cooled dramatically. He stood, saying, "We'd best get some shut-eye. Morning'll be here before we know it."

"Mr. Coltrane?"

"Hmm?"

"Thank you. For everything."

Isaiah didn't go to sleep right away. Instead, he sat with his back against a log, a small leather journal in his left hand and a pencil in his right. It was his practice to write about the things he saw and the people he met. Not daily but still frequently. He'd filled many, many journals with his careless scrawl over the past decade.

But he had yet to write about the woman who slept on the opposite side of the campfire from him. He wanted to write about her. He just couldn't seem to find the words.

She was beautiful. That went without saying.

Determined. Yes, she was that.

Headstrong. Undoubtedly.

She loved her family, and the grief she felt over the loss of her father ran deep.

She was petite but tough. He expected toughness from women who'd lived in the Rocky Mountains for years. It was less expected from a lady like Amanda who had arrived from England mere months ago.

Finally, angling the journal to capture the firelight on the paper, he wrote:

> Two days ago, I pulled a woman from the river. She was thrown from her horse after being shot at by poachers. Now I am escorting her along the Mary Mountain Trail to her place of residence in Idaho.
>
> Amanda Whitcombe is unlike any woman I have met before. I do not believe I will meet another like her again. And I will be sorry for that.

Chapter Eight

Just as Isaiah had promised, morning was there before Amanda knew it. And an extremely cold morning at that.

Despite being covered by several blankets and even sleeping in her coat, she shivered as her body came awake. She heard Isaiah moving about the campsite, preparing for the day to come and knew she needed to get up. But it was oh-so-tempting to remain hidden under the blankets for now. Thoughts of that soft bed in the room at the Yellowstone Lake House made her wish they'd spent one more night there.

Right then, Bandit poked his nose beneath her blankets, nudging her chin. She laughed as she pushed aside the covers. "All right. I'm awake." The dog wagged his tail in greeting. Amanda gave his head a pat, then reluctantly rose from the ground.

Isaiah glanced her way and gave a nod before he stoked the fire. "Morning."

"Good morning."

"Sleep good?"

She crossed her arms over her chest. "Yes. But it did turn terribly cold in the night."

"It did." As if to prove it, his breath formed a small cloud before his mouth. After setting the coffee pot over the fire, he said, "We'll push hard today. You up to it?"

"Of course."

"How's your head?"

She touched the spot. "Even better than yesterday. Not worth thinking about."

"Good."

The skillet joined the coffee pot on rocks strategically placed. This was not the first time Amanda had noticed the way Isaiah arranged stones before building a fire. On the range, the Eden's Gate cook used a gridiron over the fire, but Isaiah made do with rocks of various sizes, all of them expertly placed. Perhaps tonight, when they made camp, she would ask him to show her how to do it.

Fog, gilded by the rising sun, floated through the trees surrounding them. The scene reminded her of the paintings Roger Bernhardt had done during his visit to the park. She'd thought the works of art beautiful, but they couldn't compare to the real thing.

From across the campsite came Isaiah's voice, soft and somehow intimate. "'O Lord our Lord, how excellent is thy name in all the earth! Who hast set thy glory above the heavens.'"

Her heart fluttered in response to the words of Scripture. "Amen," she whispered.

"Hard not to believe in the Father Almighty when you see a morning like this."

His words reminded her once again of her own father, and a lump formed in her throat. Would Edward Whitcombe, the fifth Earl of Hooke, have looked at this sunrise, the fog drifting between and above the tall pines, and thought to praise God for the sight before him? Probably not. He'd believed in God, she knew, but he'd never been one to speak with others about his faith in the Creator. Apparently the same was not true of the man she'd hired to guide her back to Eden's Gate.

"Breakfast'll be ready soon, Miss Whitcombe."

She nodded, the lump in her throat keeping her silent.

———

IF ISAIAH HAD BEEN TRAVELING ALONE, he might have stayed put for a day, this being Sunday. He tried to honor the Sabbath and keep it holy. But getting this young woman back to her people, safe and sound, demanded they cover as many miles as they could over the next several days. Besides, it was Jesus Himself who'd said the Sabbath was made for man, not man for the Sabbath. It seemed to him that Lady Amanda Whitcombe had come under his protection as part of God's will. And so he would do his best to deliver her safely to Eden's Gate as soon as possible.

They ate their breakfast quickly and broke camp, setting off with the sun at their backs, the golden rays doing little to chase away the chill in the mountain air.

Despite the clear skies overhead, it smelled like it could snow. Crisp, clean, invigorating, a scent unique unto itself. Isaiah prayed he was wrong about a storm coming. He didn't want to be caught on this remote trail in a blizzard. He didn't doubt he and Bandit could survive it. He wasn't sure the same could be said for the woman the Almighty had put in his charge.

As he'd promised, they pushed hard throughout the day, stopping only when necessary to give the animals a rest and allow Amanda to do the same. Isaiah kept his eye on the heavens, thankful every minute a storm didn't materialize. By the time they made camp that night near a small lake, they were both too tired to talk. Almost too tired to eat.

Isaiah noticed that Amanda fell asleep within seconds of snuggling beneath the blankets, the firelight flickering across her face in repose. He watched her for a long while after that until weariness finally drove him to his own bedroll.

It was early in the afternoon on Tuesday when Isaiah reined in his buckskin and looked over as Amanda rode up beside him.

"It's behind us," he said.

"What is behind us?" She twisted in the saddle to see for herself.

"Yellowstone. We're out of the park."

Sadness tightened her chest, surprising her. Then again, it shouldn't surprise her to feel that way. She would never again have the opportunity to visit Yellowstone National Park. She'd seen its amazing river canyon and astounding waterfalls and beautiful lake and geysers and hot springs. She'd seen a small herd of buffalo and larger herds of elk and even a couple of moose. Overhead she'd watched hawks soaring and seen the flight of the glorious bald eagle. From a distance she'd caught sight of a grizzly bear. Sebastian had been with the ranch cowboys when they'd killed a grizzly on Eden's Gate land earlier in the summer. She was thankful the bear she saw had been far away, she out of danger from it, and it out of danger from Isaiah's rifle.

"We'll be in Idaho when we make camp tonight, and you'll be at the ranch some time tomorrow."

She moved her head from side to side, then arched her back. "I'll be thankful for a hot bath and a soft bed."

"You've done well, Miss Whitcombe."

She met his gaze and felt a slight catch in her chest. There was something in his eyes. Approval, perhaps. Respect. Perhaps even admiration.

"You did better than I thought you would," he added.

Her ire sparked—she never liked to be told someone expected her to fail—but she tamped it down. He'd actually praised her first. In fact, he admitted he'd been wrong about her. That should please rather than irritate.

A quick temper was one of her worst traits. That, along with how much she talked. Both of her brothers called her a chatterbox, and sadly, she knew it was true. She talked when she was excited, when she was angry, when she was bored. All too often, she talked when she should be silent.

Her eyes narrowed as she considered the past few days. Perhaps being with Isaiah had tempered that tendency to talk too much. Even she was surprised by the long spells she'd ridden in silence, enjoying the natural world around her. Quite unlike her.

"I like the idea of a bath and bed myself," Isaiah added, breaking into her thoughts.

She smiled in his direction. "Then you shall have both, Mr. Coltrane, and very soon from what you tell me."

With a nod, he nudged his horse forward and Amanda did the same.

They rode only a short while before she said, "It's warming up."

"We've come down a lot in elevation since this morning."

"The weather in this land has such extremes. It was terribly hot during the days this summer on the ranch. Heat like I've never experienced before. But even when the days are hot, the nights are blessedly cool. Don't you find that so?"

He sent a sideways glance in her direction, amusement in his eyes. "Yes'm, I do find it so."

I'm going to miss seeing him in the mornings. The thought was followed by a swirling sensation in her midsection, and she looked away from him, afraid he might read her emotions in her eyes.

It was true, of course. She would miss seeing him. In only a few days time, she'd grown used to his company, to the sound of his voice, to the way he sat his horse or moved around a campsite. She'd memorized his features already. The way the corner of his mouth lifted at times without becoming a true smile. The way his eyes narrowed in thought before he spoke. She'd liked his appearance on Saturday, clean-shaven, but she liked the way he looked now after three days on the trail, the shadow of a beard darkening his jaw.

Suddenly she wasn't so much eager for a bath and a bed as she was to spend more time with Isaiah Coltrane. Why had it seemed important that she return to Eden's Gate? Oh, she wished she had truly lost her memory. Or at the very least gone on pretending to have lost it. Maybe then Isaiah would have been forced to keep her with him a few days longer.

No, that wouldn't have worked. He was an honorable man, and he would have delivered her to the hotel. The touring company would have identified her, and then they would have taken responsibility for her.

"Is something troubling you?" Isaiah asked now, drawing her gaze to him once more.

She found him watching her, a frown creasing the spot between his eyebrows. Her heart did that strange little flutter. "No," she answered softly. "Nothing troubles me."

Another lie, if ever she'd told one.

Chapter Nine

It was late in the morning of the next day when Isaiah saw cattle dotting the range in a wide, long valley to the south. He assumed they were approaching Eden's Gate Ranch. Half an hour later, he saw what looked to be the ranch house, barn, and other outbuildings. Too far away for details, but they were definitely close to their destination.

Pointing ahead, he said, "Looks like you're about home."

"I shouldn't wonder."

Odd. She didn't sound pleased that the journey was almost over. In fact, she'd been unusually subdued all morning. Perhaps her thoughts had returned to the death of her father.

Movement off to his left drew Isaiah's gaze. Four horses with riders galloped in their direction. "Better stop, Miss Whitcombe." His right hand went to the butt of his rifle. He wouldn't relax until he could be certain the men didn't mean trouble.

"It's William," Amanda said, sounding more like herself. She raised an arm and waved it in a large, sweeping motion. "William! I'm back!"

The man in the lead slowed his horse while lifting a hand, commanding the others behind him to do the same. Isaiah moved his hand away from the rifle, resting it instead on his thigh. He kept his gaze focused on William Overstreet, curious to learn more about the man. Obviously he was someone who'd earned Amanda's trust. That spoke well for him. But was he more to her than a friend? That notion didn't sit well with him.

The riders drew their horses down to a walk. Then all but the rancher stopped, and William came on ahead. "Amanda. What are you doing here?"

She smiled. "That isn't a very warm welcome."

He released a short laugh. "Sorry. No, it wasn't. But you weren't expected to return for another ten days."

"I know, but I grew homesick."

William's gaze moved beyond Amanda to Isaiah.

Isaiah couldn't see the question in the other man's eyes, but he felt it. He nudged Buck forward, at the same time giving the brim of his hat a bump with his knuckles, pushing it back on his head. "Mr. Overstreet, I'm Isaiah Coltrane."

William nodded.

"Miss Whitcombe hired me to guide her back to Eden's Gate."

"It's a long story, William." Amanda brought her horse once again to Isaiah's side. "And I promise to tell you absolutely everything. But I would dearly love to get to the ranch first. It's been a long trip, and Mr. Coltrane and I are both tired and thirsty. I've promised Mr. Coltrane a bed and a bath, and I'm sure Mr. Kincaid will have something wonderful to feed us. I'm tired of jerky and salt pork and beans which is what we've dined on for several days."

Isaiah resisted the smile tugging at his mouth. There was the Amanda he'd missed hearing from today. Silence didn't suit her, and when he was with her, he didn't want it either. He liked the tone of her voice, the hint of England in her accent. He liked the zest with which she met each new day, each new situation. To be honest, he even liked when he got under her skin and her temper sparked. He might not find that amusing if her anger lingered, but that hadn't happened over the course of their brief acquaintance.

"Men." William twisted in his saddle to look behind. "You go on without me. I'm going to ride to the house with Miss Amanda."

"Right, boss," one of them responded. Then the cowboys turned their horses back in the direction they'd come and cantered off.

The three remaining riders headed in the direction of the ranch house, Amanda between the two men.

"Is Mrs. Adler well? Is Roger off painting today? I can't wait to talk to him about Yellowstone. I didn't see everything he saw, of course. I wasn't in the park long enough. But Mr. Coltrane and I rode through some amazing country. It was just a trail we followed. Not a road. Not many visitors to the park get to see what we saw. We even saw a grizzly bear from a distance, and I thought of the one Sebastian and Jocelyn and the others shot on your ranch this summer. I'm glad Mr. Coltrane didn't have to kill the one we saw. After all, his job in the park is to catch poachers to stop them from hunting the big game. Isn't that right, Mr. Coltrane?"

Smothering another smile, he answered, "It is, Miss Whitcombe." A surreptitious glance in her direction brought his gaze into contact with William's. He caught the unmistakeable hint of a smirk on his mouth and believed the two of them were destined to become friends. Although, first he would need to explain how he came to bring Amanda along the Mary Mountain Trail in Yellowstone and back to Eden's Gate, just the two of them.

———

AMANDA LOOKED around the supper table that night, and her heart ached for those whose chairs were empty. She keenly felt the absence of her father, as well as her brother and his wife. But at least she knew she would see Sebastian and Jocelyn in the spring when she returned to England. But she wouldn't see her father again this side of heaven.

At that thought, those infernal tears welled up, blurring her vision.

Seated next to her, Roger Bernhardt—fair-haired with piercing blue eyes—whispered, "Are you all right, Amanda?" Trust him to notice her mood. Roger took in everything. Always observant. It must be the artist in him, the way he watched people, the way he noticed the world around him.

"I'm all right," she answered softly. "Just thinking of Father."

"I'm sorry, my dear. I know you feel the loss keenly."

Blinking away her tears, she nodded, no longer trusting herself to speak until this wave of sorrow passed. Instead, she looked toward the head of the table where William sat, Isaiah on his right. The two men were deep in a conversation of their own. Amanda wished she could eavesdrop on their conversation.

Roger passed her a serving bowl of baked squash. "Mr. Coltrane is an interesting man. Quite different from what I expected when I saw him ride in with you."

"Yes." She spooned the buttered squash, sprinkled with brown sugar, onto her plate next to the slice of roast beef and gravy.

"I had an opportunity to talk with him this afternoon," he added.

She wondered if a better word might be interrogate. Both Roger and William would, undoubtedly, try to fill the role of her absent older brother. That was an unpleasant thought. She didn't need or want either of them seeking to control her.

Isaiah chose that moment to glance in her direction. His smile was fleeting, there and gone, but she felt it to her core. All other thoughts fled, and she returned the smile, hers lingering on her lips.

"Amanda." Roger drew out her name.

"What?" She set aside the serving bowl.

"I realize he rescued you from the river, but don't

romanticize the experience. Don't romanticize the man."

Eyes widening, she turned her gaze on Roger. "Whatever do you mean?"

"You know very well what I mean."

"Don't you dare treat me like a child, Roger Bernhardt."

"Sebastian would say—"

"Sebastian is not here."

"No, but he—"

"Roger, don't be a goose." She placed her fingertips on the back of his wrist, his hand resting on the table. "You are my brother's closest friend, and I adore you. I have always adored you. But I have no intention of falling under your protection just because Sebastian returned to England. I am not required to follow the rules set by society. Not while I am on this ranch. Not while I am in America, the land of the free and the home of the brave. I will not allow you to censure my every thought or action."

"That wasn't my intention."

"Perhaps it wasn't your intention, but it's what you were doing." She glanced in Isaiah's direction once again. "Besides, Mr. Coltrane is leaving in a day or two. So you needn't worry what I might think of him after that."

As she returned her attention to the food on her plate, she felt a strange ache in her heart. Not an ache for the people she loved who were no longer present, but an ache for the man—a man who had been a stranger to her less than a week before—who would soon ride out of her life, once and for all.

———

It hadn't taken Isaiah long to discover that Amanda was highly regarded by the two other men at the table, men who were good friends of Amanda's brother, Sebastian Whitcombe. Unusual perhaps—to find such close friendships between a British earl, an American rancher, and the son of a London shopkeeper—but made obvious in the discussions that took place during the meal.

When Isaiah first joined the other three in the dining room, he'd wondered if there might be something more ardent between William and Amanda. They appeared well suited for each other. But as he'd conversed with the rancher and observed the interactions around the table, he'd ruled out romantic affection. William sounded and behaved far more like an older brother than a suitor. Just as Amanda had described him. The same was soon proven true about Roger as well. Both of these men would fight to protect and shelter Amanda. They cared deeply for her. But not as lovers.

Odd, how arriving at that conclusion seemed to brighten the evening.

Chapter Ten

I saiah was saddling Buck in the shade on the west side of the barn when one of the Eden's Gate ranch hands strode around the corner.

"The boss around?" the young cowboy asked him.

"Sorry. I haven't seen him."

Jake Foster, the ranch foreman, walked over from one of the corrals. "What is it, Logan?"

"Rustlers are back. They hit the Jackson place last night."

"I'll find William." Jake turned on his heel and headed toward the house.

Isaiah returned his attention to Logan. "Have you been having trouble with rustlers for long?"

"They've hit several ranches this summer. They didn't get any Overstreet cattle this year, but not because they ain't tried. Might not be as lucky this time."

Isaiah didn't know exactly how much land made up Eden's Gate, but it was a lot. A lot of ground and a lot of cattle to keep an eye on. If the rustlers knew what they were doing, how hard could it be to make off with some of the herd? Rustlers, like poachers, were willing to take risks if it meant easy gain. Beef on the hoof brought a pretty price.

He patted Buck's neck before taking a step away from the horse. The back door off the kitchen closed hard, and he watched William, followed by Jake, striding toward them.

"What can you tell me, Logan?"

The young man gave a quick report of what he'd seen for himself on the south range and what he'd been told by cowboys from the Jackson ranch.

William muttered something beneath his breath before saying, "I'd hoped we were done with them. At least for this year."

"I reckon we're not," Jake said.

"Better get word to the rest of the boys." William glanced up, judging the height of the sun. "Logan, you head east. Jake and I'll go south."

Isaiah said, "Could you use my help?"

William faced him. "I thought you were headed back to Montana."

"Nothing back home that can't wait a day or two longer. If I can be of help, I'd like to."

"Well then, I won't turn you down. Be glad to hire you on. The more eyes we've got on the ground, the better. And from what Amanda tells me, we could make use of your tracking skills. These rustlers have slipped away every time they've hit the ranches over the last couple of months. They cover their trail like nothing

I've seen before. I'd like to catch them. Put an end to their thieving ways, once and for all."

"I'll do my best to see that happens."

William stuck out a hand. "Glad to have you with us."

The two men shook on it.

Upon Isaiah's arrival yesterday, William had given him a guest room in the house. He'd been grateful for the hospitality. However, he didn't expect that to continue.

As if reading his thoughts, William said, "You can keep the room you're in. With any luck, you won't be here more than a few days."

Isaiah pushed back his hat with his knuckles. "Don't think that would be right. Last night was one thing after escorting Miss Whitcombe home from the park. This here's another matter. If I'm working for you, I'll bunk with the other hired hands."

William nodded, perhaps knowing Isaiah's decision was for the best.

Isaiah turned to his horse and tightened the cinch before dropping the stirrup into place. Gathering the reins in hand, he gave a whistle that brought Bandit to attention. Then he stepped into the saddle. As he tugged on his hat, making sure it was secure on his head, the screened door slammed closed again, and Amanda hurried toward them.

"Is it true?" she asked. "The rustlers are back?"

Rather than answering himself, Isaiah twisted to look at William, who was now astride his own horse.

"It's true." William rode closer. "Isaiah's going to help us track them. See if we can put an end to it."

She shaded her eyes from the sun with both hands as she looked up at him. "Thank you, Mr. Coltrane." She took a step forward and placed her hand flat on Buck's neck. "This is more than kind of you."

Strange. It almost felt as if he'd offered to stay to track rustlers because of her. And mercy, she was a sight to behold with the morning light falling over her like that, gilding her dark hair. Even bedraggled as he'd pulled her out of the river a week ago, he'd known she was pretty. But this morning, there was something—

He gave a light pull on the reins, causing Buck to back up a few steps, seeking to remove himself from whatever spell she'd cast over him.

"All right," William said. "Let's ride, men."

"Bandit, come." Isaiah fell in behind William and Jake as they headed out of the Eden's Gate barnyard.

AMANDA REMAINED WHERE SHE WAS, watching the three men ride away.

He isn't leaving yet. The thought brought unexpected delight.

Isaiah wasn't headed for Montana. Not yet. Not today. Instead, he had hired on to work for William, helping them hunt down the rustlers who'd plagued the ranches from here down to Pocatello over the summer. If anyone could find them, Isaiah could. She believed it with all her heart.

When she turned around, she saw Mrs. Adler observing her from the front porch. Rather than go into the house through the kitchen, she walked in the direction of the housekeeper. "The rustlers are back."

"So I heard." The woman crossed her arms over her ample bosom. "Miss Whitcombe, you need to mind yourself."

Amanda stopped before climbing the steps. "Whatever do you mean?"

The woman cocked an eyebrow. "You know good and well what I mean, and don't go pretending otherwise. It's bad enough you hired him to bring you alone out of the park. All those days and nights, just the two of you. Heaven knows what could've gone wrong. Why, Miss Joss would have a conniption fit if I let you get yourself into trouble with a man like that."

"A man like *what*, exactly."

Mrs. Adler huffed in answer.

Over the course of the summer, Amanda had learned the housekeeper was fiercely protective of those she loved. And, for that matter, for anyone who fell under her care. That now included Amanda, especially since Sebastian's and Jocelyn's departure.

"Did you know Mr. Coltrane studied at Georgetown University?" Amanda went up the steps to the porch. "His father hoped he would become a lawyer one day, but that isn't the life he chose."

"Lawyers. I don't have much good to say about them either."

Amanda hooked an arm with Mrs. Adler. "Could you please give him a chance? He saved my life from poachers and the river. He escorted me safely back to the ranch and behaved as a gentleman the entire way. Nothing inappropriate happened. Not ever. And now he is doing William a good turn."

"I guess if you put it that way," the older woman muttered.

Amanda laughed. "I do put it that way."

Still arm-in-arm, they moved toward the front door. Only there did Amanda release the housekeeper so they could go into the house in single file.

While Mrs. Adler returned to whatever house-keeping duties awaited her, Amanda climbed the stairs to her bedroom. Silence awaited her there. The same silence that blanketed every room in the house now that the men were out on the range.

"I should have gone with them," she said aloud as she crossed the bedroom to the window.

The view from there was of gently rolling land, stretching all the way to the small town of Gibeon. Not that she could see the town from this vantage point, but she knew it was there. Most Sundays over the summer they'd attended church services in Gibeon—William, Sebastian, Roger, Jocelyn, and Amanda. Most of the cowboys and Mrs. Adler went to church in town as well.

She wondered if Isaiah would go to church with them on Sunday. But, of course, he would. He was the sort of man who quoted Scripture on a Sunday, even when in the remotest part of the wilderness. That was something else Mrs. Adler would like about him, if she'd give him a chance.

A frown crinkled her brow. Why was it important to

her that the other woman like Isaiah, that she approved of him? It wasn't as if he planned to stay on Eden's Gate. This wasn't his home, and it wasn't her home either. And yet it mattered to her. It felt important that others in her life like and appreciate him the way she did.

She turned and went to the small writing desk. She'd written many letters while seated here over the course of the summer. Perhaps writing another would help take her thoughts off the game scout now riding with William and the other ranch hands.

---

5 September 1895

Dearest Sebastian and Jocelyn,

I hope this letter finds you well and settling into life at Hooke Manor as the new earl and countess. I send you my love, along with the same to Adam and Eliza.

As you know, I decided to take my planned excursion into Yellowstone National Park soon after you departed, knowing it would be my last opportunity to do so. Everything I saw on my trip was incredibly beautiful, as has been true of so much of what we have seen in this country. Breathtaking sights. Even more so than what Roger captured on his canvasses during his stay in the park. However, I soon discovered (as others, including you, warned me) that my heart was not ready to be with a group of strangers. And so, I cut my tour short and returned to Eden's Gate yesterday.

I did have one adventure in the park that I did not plan on. I became separated from the tour group while we were transitioning from one camp-site to another. One thing led to another, and I ended up needing to be rescued from the river by a game scout hired by the army. There is much more to the story, of course, but it shall have to wait until we are together again because the explanation is long. Besides, the telling in person is much better than attempting to write it, and I shall very much enjoy seeing your faces as I describe it all to you. All you need to know for now is that I did not drown in the river, and I am well and whole and safely back under the watchful eyes of Mrs. Adler and William.

I returned to more excitement. It seems the rustlers you sought earlier this summer have returned. William is determined to put an end to it, as I'm sure are the other ranchers. He is out hunting for them even as I write this letter. In fact, the game scout I mentioned who rescued me in the park has been hired to help track the thieves. Quite fortuitous, is it not, that he should be available. I suppose I shall have to tell you how that came about as well, but it will wait for another time.

Now that I am back at the ranch, I will begin working again with Ebony while the weather is fine. Hopefully we will not have an early start of winter, something William has mentioned as a possibility more than once.

Do write to me often and tell me of everything you are doing. I am not sorry I remained in America until spring. But I do regret not being there as Jocelyn is introduced to society as your new bride. I'm sure there is more than one hopeful young woman and her mother with broken hearts.

Your loving sister,
Amanda

Chapter Eleven

On Sunday morning, Amanda rode beside William in the surrey as he drove the rig toward Gibeon. Roger and Mrs. Adler sat on the seat behind them, and several cowboys, along with Isaiah, rode their horses off to the side, avoiding the dust thrown up by the surrey's wheels. Jake Foster and the remainder of the Eden's Gate ranch hands had stayed behind to protect the cattle. After three days of searching, the rustlers hadn't been caught nor their trail discovered, to the consternation of all the ranchers in the area.

In town, Truman Blankenship stood at the top of the steps of Gibeon Chapel, greeting the members of his congregation as they approached the church, some walking to the church from elsewhere in town, many arriving by buggy, wagon, and on horseback. William gave the reverend a wave as he guided the horse to the shady side of the white clapboard building.

Sebastian had once commented to Amanda about the reverend's youthful appearance and how, at first, he'd doubted the man's ability to shepherd his flock. But the good reverend was older than he looked, and he preached powerful sermons, Sunday after Sunday.

Now, Reverend Blankenship greeted her warmly at the door. "We've missed you, Miss Whitcombe."

"Thank you, Reverend. It's good to be back." As she stepped into the small narthex, she heard Isaiah introduce himself to the pastor. Her heart skipped a beat, then her pulse sped up. She hadn't realized he was so close behind her.

She'd seen little of Isaiah since Thursday morning. He'd moved his belongings out of the guest room and into the bunkhouse. He, William, and the cowboys had ridden out the last two mornings while the sun was a mere promise on the horizon, and they'd arrived back as gloaming fell over the earth. With all the men out on the range—with the exception of Roger and Mr. Kincaid—Amanda had spent her days with her horse, lost in her own thoughts. No wonder the sound of an unexpected voice, so close to her, made her heart quicken.

But was that really the reason?

William—always the gentleman—took her arm and steered her toward the Overstreet pew on the right side of the center aisle. She settled in between him and Mrs. Adler. It took great resolve not to try to see where Isaiah sat for the service, but somehow she managed to keep her eyes focused straight ahead.

Reverend Blankenship spoke that morning on the importance of family, both earthly and eternal. He explained how when a person trusts in Christ for salvation, he or she is adopted into the family of God. "We are no longer orphans, begging for scraps in this world. We are sons and daughters of the King of the universe. Of God Most High. From the moment of salvation, we are surrounded by brothers and sisters in the Lord, both here in our little town of Gibeon and to the farthest corners of this earth. Wherever the Gospel has been received, we will find brothers and sisters. And they will remain our brothers and sisters throughout eternity."

I have no father and no mother in this world. That makes me an orphan. As that thought whirled inside her, stinging her heart, the pastor's words rushed to replace it. *But I'm a daughter of the King. I'm a child of God Most High. I am not an orphan.* Tears sprang to her eyes, but they came with a sense of joy. *Thank You, Father. And please, tell my earthly father that I'll be all right.*

FROM HIS VANTAGE point on the left side of the sanctuary, Isaiah was able to see Amanda's profile. In truth, he'd spent much of the service observing her, even as he listened to Reverend Blankenship's message. His spirit saw a change come over her as the pastor brought his sermon to a close. It might not make sense to others, but he'd swear she was feeling lighter, freer. It was as if a burden had been lifted off her shoulders.

Thank You, Lord, for Your mercy, for whatever You took from her.

The congregation rose to sing one of Isaiah's favorite hymns, accompanied on the piano by a gray-haired woman.

"'Rock of Ages, cleft for me, / let me hide myself in thee; / let the water and the blood, / from thy wounded side which flowed, / be of sin the double cure, / save from wrath and make me pure.'"

As always, the lyrics did something in his heart as he sang them. They filled him with wonder and thanksgiving. Wonder that God had cared enough for him to send His Son to die. Thanksgiving that his sins had been covered by the blood of the Savior and made him pure before the throne.

"'Not the labors of my hands / can fulfill thy law's demands; / could my zeal no respite know, / could my tears forever flow, / all for sin could not atone; / thou must save, and thou alone.'"

Isaiah Coltrane was no stranger to hard work, and he was willing to do it. But it was good to remember that nothing he did on this side of the grave could make him good enough or clean enough to fulfill the law or atone for his sins. He needed Christ every hour.

"'While I draw this fleeting breath, / when mine eyes shall close in death, / when I soar to worlds unknown, / see thee on thy judgment throne, / Rock of Ages, cleft for me, / let me hide myself in thee.'"

The hymn ended with a lengthy, "Amen."

From the pulpit, the reverend intoned, "Go in peace."

Isaiah hung back as members of the congregation began to file out of the church, conversations springing up between neighbors and friends as they walked. He watched as Reverend Blankenship spoke to members of his flock, slowly making his way toward the sanctuary exit and finally out onto the front stoop of the church. It was there that Isaiah spoke to him.

"Fine sermon, reverend. I appreciated it."

"Thank you, Mr. Coltrane. I'm glad you could be with us."

It impressed Isaiah that the pastor remembered his name. Many wouldn't have. Not after a quick introduction well over an hour before.

"I hope you'll join us again."

"If I'm still in the area on a Sunday, I'll be sure to be here." He settled his hat on his head, gave the pastor a nod, then went down the steps.

Amanda and Mrs. Adler were seated in the Overstreet surrey by the time Isaiah got to his horse. However, William and the Eden's Gate cowboys were deep in conversation with a group of men Isaiah didn't know. It didn't take much to guess the subject was rustlers and stolen cattle. It might be a discussion that lasted awhile.

He took Buck's reins and led the horse toward the surrey. He tugged the brim of his hat, making eye contact with each of the women. "Fine sermon," he said to Amanda.

"Yes." A smile blossomed on her mouth, and again he thought how she appeared lighter in a way he couldn't define.

He glanced toward the men whose voices had grown louder. "They don't sound happy."

Amanda frowned. "Jocelyn, William's sister, explained to me how deeply these thefts affect the ranchers. With so many cattle on the range, I couldn't understand the impact of twenty-five or fifty or even a hundred cattle here and there. But each cow, each calf, matters a great deal to those men."

Isaiah wasn't a cattle rancher, but he understood the economics of such enterprises. The trouble for them was real, even for the wealthiest among them, and it frustrated him that he hadn't found a trail to follow over the last few days. Maybe the rustlers didn't plan to strike again. Maybe they'd moved out of the valley altogether with their ill-gotten gains. But he should be able to find some sign of them. The wind couldn't have blown away all traces of horses and cattle. Tracks had to be out there. He just needed to find them. Hopefully before the rustlers sold the cattle to some unsuspecting buyers.

"Will you stay on, Mr. Coltrane?"

Amanda's question pulled his attention back to her. The way she looked at him now made him want to reply in the affirmative.

"William and the others need your help. This is so dreadfully unfortunate for them. But I know you can find the thieves if you are given enough time."

"I'd like to try to find them, Miss Whitcombe."

It wasn't as if there were any pressing demands awaiting him in Montana. Getting plenty of firewood chopped for winter. Hunting and fishing to increase his food stores. And he needed to return the pinto to Paddy Muldoon. Paddy would be looking for the little horse soon, expecting Isaiah to have returned to his cabin. Maybe he should have let Amanda purchase a new mount while in Yellowstone. Then he wouldn't have any reason to go home. Not now at any rate.

"I'm glad," she said, another one of her beautiful smiles following her words.

He wanted to earn that smile. He couldn't remember a time in his life when something mattered to him as much as the desire to deliver on the hope and trust he saw in her eyes.

Chapter Twelve

A manda had no intention of being left behind when the men rode out the next morning. She rose early, dressed for a day in the saddle, and ate her breakfast even before her host appeared in the dining room.

William grinned when he saw her. "I take it you plan to join us."

"I do." She tried to mimic the look Jocelyn used to give him when she was determined to have her own way.

A chuckle rumbled in his chest as he crossed to the sideboard to fill a plate with eggs and sausage along with a fat slice of toasted bread slathered with butter. He carried the plate and a full cup of Mr. Kincaid's excellent coffee to the table. Once settled, he closed his eyes for a moment—she assumed for a prayer of thanks—before picking up his fork.

"I suppose you heard," he said, "that Mr. Coltrane has agreed to stay on for the time being."

"I believed he would if you asked him."

William took a bite of eggs. After swallowing, he continued, "We may not have caught the rustlers, but I could see his skills as a tracker. The man knows what he's doing. I'm thankful he's staying. If the rustlers left any signs of where they went, he'll find them if anyone can."

Strange, how personal those words were to her. As if she'd earned the praise, not Isaiah. But she didn't deserve praise. All she'd done was fall into a river. "He saved me."

"What?" William asked, a puzzled expression turned in her direction.

She hadn't realized she'd spoken the words aloud. Embarrassed, she gave her head a shake. "Nothing. I was . . . I was thinking of something else."

His puzzlement changed to a frown. "Or *someone* else."

"Whatever do you mean?"

"You know what I mean, Amanda. My impressions of Mr. Coltrane are positive, and his reputation is good among men in the area. I checked. But if I thought you'd formed any sort of attachment to him during the time you spent together—"

Why must everyone warn her about her feelings for Isaiah? First Roger. Then Mrs. Adler. Now William. She lifted her chin defiantly. "I have done no such thing. Mr. Coltrane is a capable guide, and I was thankful for the service he provided, escorting me back to Eden's Gate."

"Sebastian entrusted you to my care, Amanda."

"I do not need a keeper."

"That's not my intent. But—"

"William, you have become as dear to me as my own brother. But please allow me the same freedom as you allowed Jocelyn when she was with you."

"My sister worked with our father from a young age. She ran the shipping company after our father's death and lived alone in the big city. Not to mention she is seven years older than you. Your life has been much more sheltered than hers ever was."

What William said was true. Her life had been sheltered. But she was not a child nor was she a hot house flower, and she didn't want to be told what to do or where to go or who she could or could not be fond of.

Fond of. Was that all it was with Isaiah? Fondness.

"Amanda, Isaiah Coltrane lives a solitary life in the mountains of Montana. He doesn't own much more than a patch of land with a one-room cabin on it, a horse, and a dog. He told me so himself. And as you said, he did you a service. But you mustn't let yourself feel anything more than grateful that he helped you in a time of need."

"Why are you even saying all of that?" She placed the napkin beside her plate and rose to her feet. "Really, William. You are quite frustrating." With a small toss of her head, she left the dining room and headed for the barn.

The September sun had yet to climb above the Tetons in the east, but daylight still spilled over the barn-yard. Chickens clucked in the coop, and horses munched on hay that had been tossed into the corrals.

One of the cowboys leaned against the bunkhouse, smoking a cigarette, while others saddled and bridled their mounts.

Amanda entered the barn where Bella, Jocelyn's bay mare, stood in her stall. As she brought the horse out, she recalled William's words about how sheltered her life had been.

At Hooke Manor, she wouldn't have brushed a horse herself or saddled it herself. There would have been a groom to do all of that for her. She would have informed a servant when she wanted to go riding, and she'd have found her mount waiting for her at the appropriate time. She hadn't known then how much pleasure could be found in brushing a horse's coat, whisking away dirt and flecks of hay. It was a simple thing but she loved it. She hadn't known she could saddle and bridle a horse without assistance. Not until she'd come to America. There was satisfaction to be found in doing for oneself.

How could she explain any of that to William? He'd never been told he couldn't do something. He'd never been kept from doing hard, manual work. And he certainly didn't know what it was like to be female in a male-dominated society.

She closed her eyes as she leaned her forehead against Bella's neck, her thoughts traveling across the ocean, remembering one of the last supper parties held at Hooke Manor before she, Sebastian, and Roger departed for America. She saw herself as she'd played hostess, charming the man to her left and then the one to her right. She knew all the ways to use feminine wiles to get her own way. She'd deployed them often, including with her father. But she didn't want to live that way. She would rather be open and honest with the people around her. She didn't want to manipulate and pretend to be something she was not or to feel something she didn't feel. She wanted to participate in life.

The clearing of a throat jerked her to the present. She straightened and looked toward the barn door. Isaiah stood there, the sunlight streaming in from behind him.

"Good morning, Miss Whitcombe."

"Mr. Coltrane."

He moved a few steps deeper into the barn. "Are you planning to ride with us this morning?"

"Yes." She readied herself to hear him ask why or say she shouldn't go.

Instead, he said, "Always good to have another pair of eyes."

Her heart warmed, and she admitted to herself that she was, indeed, quite fond of Mr. Coltrane.

THAT MORNING, Isaiah pointed his horse toward the northeast. With him were William, Amanda, Tom Flores, Logan Coe, and Rocky Turner. Yesterday, riding back from Gibeon, Isaiah had studied the mountain range in the distance, and a thought occurred to him. If the thieves took the cattle higher up those foothills and took care to sweep away signs of where they'd gone, they would be able to stay hidden in the trees as they drove the cattle north. They would be like poachers in the park. Almost invisible.

No one talked as they cantered across the grazing land. Bandit ran slightly ahead and off to Isaiah's left. The dog could easily keep up this pace for eight to ten miles if necessary, but Isaiah and the others would need to slow before then. They would be looking for signs the rustlers hadn't been able to disguise, and his gut told him the signs would be there. According to William, their searches had covered the south and the west. No one had thought to ride up into the hills.

As they closed in on his destination, Isaiah reined in with his left hand while raising his right to indicate the others should do the same. Soon after they slowed to a walk, William rode up beside him.

Isaiah pulled Buck to a stop. "Let's spread out from here. If they've moved cattle through those trees, there'll be signs of them. Nothing they could do to hide it all."

William pushed his hat back on his head. "Where would they take them from up there?"

"If it were me—" Isaiah pointed. "—I'd take cattle over that mountain and straight through to Montana, sticking as close to the Yellowstone border as I could manage."

"We've spent our time looking the other direction. More ways to get them to market. More places to hide a small herd."

Isaiah gave his head a small shake. "No guarantee I'm right. It's just a hunch I've got."

"I hope your hunch is right." William twisted in his

saddle. "Rocky, you go with Isaiah. Tom and Logan, you two stay together. Amanda, you come with me."

Isaiah felt a sting of disappointment, only then realizing he'd hoped to have Amanda riding at his side once again. He missed the lilt of her voice as she talked of one thing or another. He hadn't spent more than a few moments in her company since the night of their arrival at the ranch. Their exchange yesterday after the church service had been equally brief. He wanted more time with her. He wanted—

But what he wanted wasn't a good idea. He knew it, and he was pretty sure William Overstreet knew it too.

Chapter Thirteen

I saiah rode slowly through the forest of lodgepole and ponderosa pines, Douglas fir and quaking aspen, climbing ever higher up the mountainside, his eyes searching the ground and underbrush for telltale signs of the rustlers. They'd been in this area. He was convinced of it. But so far, the only tracks he'd recognized were from small forest creatures and one big cat. Mountain lions were solitary, elusive animals that preferred to avoid contact with humans, but it was possible a hungry cat wanted to find the cattle almost as much as Isaiah did.

He couldn't see Rocky at present, but he heard him moving through the forest, pine needles crunching beneath his horse's hooves. Tom and Logan had gone even farther to the south while William and Amanda were somewhere farther north of him. Too far away for sounds of their search to reach him.

Up ahead, Bandit stopped and lifted his nose to sniff the air.

"What do you smell, boy?" Isaiah said softly.

The dog lowered his head again and moved forward, a little faster now than before.

Isaiah pressed his heels to Buck's side. "Rocky, Bandit's got the scent of something."

He perceived no need to move stealthily. It wasn't the same as trying to catch poachers in the act. They wouldn't find rustlers in these mountains today. Not if his hunch was right about where they'd taken the cattle and how they'd moved them over the past months.

After about ten more minutes of climbing, the incline growing steeper, the trees thinning somewhat, he saw the first signs of the thieves. The hooves of many cattle had carved an unmistakable trail in the earth.

"You were right," Rocky said as he rode up beside Isaiah.

"Hmm." Isaiah dismounted and followed the edge of the trail. After a moment, he squatted on his heels and ran his fingers over some prints. "I'd guess there's six to eight of them. And I'd say they've used this trail a lot." He stood. "I'll follow it north. William'll see it soon for himself, if he hasn't already. Why don't you follow it south and see if you and the others can discover where they began the climb up here?"

"I'll do it." Rocky reined his horse and rode off.

Isaiah leaned over to give Bandit a few strokes on the side of his head. "Good boy." Then he mounted up and turned Buck north. He nudged the horse into a trot, his gaze locked on the ground ahead of him.

WHILE WILLIAM DISMOUNTED and walked to and fro, his gaze locked on the ground, Amanda allowed herself to relax and enjoy the beauty of their surroundings. To her right, mountains rose in resplendent glory, touching the sky with their blue-purple peaks. To her left, the rocky earth fell away, providing an overlook of a deep, narrow canyon, sprinkled here and there with the colors of early fall.

"Isaiah was right," William said. "This is definitely where they were."

She smiled. Of course Isaiah was right. She twisted in the saddle to say as much to him.

A cry, similar to a woman's anguished scream, ripped through the momentary stillness. The voice of the untamed wilderness—beautiful, chilling, and impossible to forget. Bella whinnied her alarm. Off balance, Amanda grabbed for the saddle horn, but it was too late. The mare was already on her hind legs, her front legs striking out at an unseen threat. Amanda flew from the saddle and hit the ground hard. Her breath rushed out as she slid on the shale toward the cliff's edge. She grasped at anything that might provide an anchor, but nothing held. Over the side she went. Perhaps she screamed or perhaps it was still the scream of a wild animal that she heard.

A rifle fired at the same moment she hit something solid, abruptly stopping her descent. The breath rushed out of her a second time.

ISAIAH HADN'T BEEN on the move long when three bone-chilling sounds rent the air, followed soon after by the report of a rifle. He recognized each of the three screams, despite them happening almost simultaneously. One was the shrill howl of a mountain lion. The second that of a terrified horse. The third was the cry of a woman. A cry he'd heard before.

Amanda!

He kicked Buck into a gallop, ice flowing in his veins. The horse zigged and zagged through the trees, following the trail the cattle had carved out before them. Just as the trees ended, he saw the bay mare Amanda had ridden racing toward him, riderless. He made no attempt to capture it. With any luck, Rocky would have heard the rifle fire and be riding in this direction once again. Maybe he would catch the mare.

Then, at the top of the ridge, he saw William's horse, reins dragging the ground. A heartbeat later, he saw the man lying on his belly. But there was no sign of Amanda. Or the mountain lion. His throat went dry.

William pushed up at the sound of Isaiah's approach. "Hurry!" he shouted. "We need a rope."

Isaiah came off Buck with the coiled lariat already in his hand. He slid to a stop at the edge of the ridge, a sharp drop-off before him. His heart nearly stopped, too, when his gaze found Amanda, clinging to a narrow ledge about twenty feet below him. Small rocks and shale skittered from beneath his boots to tumble down the cliff, some of them striking Amanda on the head.

"Are you hurt?" he called down to her.

"I … I don't think so."

"Hold on. Stay as still as you can."

William was on his feet now. "Amanda, we'll lower a rope to you and pull you up."

She nodded.

Isaiah tied a knot in one end of the rope for her to hold onto. After making certain it was tight, he tossed the rope down the side of the rocky face to her. She reached for it, then returned her hand to the shrub that had become her anchor.

"Hold still," he repeated. "I'll get the rope to you." He pulled the rope up and tried again. This time it landed on her shoulder. "Make sure you've got a good grip."

"I've got it."

With Isaiah and William holding onto the rope, they began to pull. But only a moment later, Amanda released a small cry and let go. Both men stumbled backward, then rushed together to the edge and looked down.

"It's my right wrist," she said, pain in her voice. "I must have sprained it. I can't . . . I can't get a good grip on the rope."

Isaiah exchanged a look with William. "You'll need to lower me down. I'll tie the rope around her and you can pull her up. I'll wait on the ledge until you can pull me up too." He went to his horse and brought Buck closer to the edge. Once there, he secured the rope around the saddle horn.

Bandit barked, perhaps expressing his disapproval.

"Quiet."

The dog sat and looked away.

Isaiah gave Buck's neck a pat. "I'm counting on you, fella."

He walked to the edge, the rope flowing through his gloved hand. There he gave a nod to William who gripped the lariat, as if already trying to bear Isaiah's weight.

"She'll be all right," Isaiah said, turning his back toward the drop-off as he looped the rope behind him. He wished he felt as confident as he sounded.

Leaning against the rope at his back, he walked himself down the side of the cliff. He talked to Amanda as he went, hoping to reassure her. She, on the other hand, was unusually silent. And that worried him.

HEART IN THROAT, Amanda watched as Isaiah drew closer to her. The ledge that had stopped her descent was narrow. Too narrow for him. He was a tall man with broad shoulders.

"I'm here," he said, voice gentle. "You'll be all right."

She nodded, trying to hide the terror she felt. She wasn't an enthusiast of great heights, not even when they afforded such spectacular scenery.

Kneeling near her on the ledge, Isaiah removed the rope from around his back, then drew it around her waist and knotted it securely. "Hold on with both hands. I know you've hurt your wrist, but grip as best you can. Let William and Buck pull you while you use your legs to walk up the face of the mountain as you go. Just put one foot in front of the other. You can do it."

She nodded again.

He looked toward the ridge. "She's ready, William. Tighten the rope. Give her a chance to stand."

Stand? Her legs felt like jelly. How on earth was she to stand?

But somehow she did, Isaiah's hand on the small of her back steadying her. As the rope grew more taut, she tightened her grip. Needles of pain shot up her right arm from her sprained wrist but she stifled a cry.

As she took her first step, she said, "You have rescued me again, Mr. Coltrane."

"Let's not make a habit of it, Miss Whitcombe."

"Agreed."

One foot in front of the other. That's all she had to do. Put one foot in front of the other.

Although it seemed an eternity, she knew it didn't take long before her head rose above the edge of the cliff and William grabbed hold beneath her arms, pulling her the remainder of the way onto solid ground. Hugging him, she couldn't hold back the cry of relief as she had the one from pain.

"Thank God," William said.

"Amen," she whispered.

He drew back to look her in the face. "Sebastian will kill me if anything happens to you."

He removed his gloves long enough to untie the knot in the rope that had kept her safe. Gloves on again, he rose and led Buck close to the edge a second time. There, he tossed the rope to Isaiah.

As much as Amanda hated the idea of staring down into the deep ravine, she had to know what was happening. On her belly, she scooted forward in time to see Isaiah grab the rope. But the sight caused her breath to catch again. The ledge *was* too narrow for him. How had he managed to cling to the mountainside while he waited for the rope to be tossed down to him? Holding her breath, she watched as he pulled himself upright.

"I'm ready, William."

"All right, Buck. Back. Back, boy."

It was nearly as frightening to watch Isaiah climb up the face of the cliff as it had been to experience it for herself. Her gaze shifted to the rope off to her right, watching as it inched steadily but surely over the edge. She heard William talking to the horse and seemed to feel the weight they pulled in her own chest.

At the moment she looked down again, when Isaiah was about halfway up, the wall beneath his boots gave way. Rocks—large and small—fell, rolling and tumbling and crashing into the bottom of the ravine. His feet went out from under him, and his shoulder slammed into the cliff. Somehow he kept hold of the rope even as he slipped downward, all the way to that narrow ledge—and then below it.

She cried out in horror as he dangled in the air, hands gripping the rope. Could she ever forgive herself if something happened to him because of her?

William arrived beside her. "Isaiah!"

The only response was grunts and groans as Isaiah worked his way onto the ledge where he lay on one side.

"Isaiah!" William shouted again.

"You're going to have to drag me up. I think I busted my ankle."

Amanda sucked in a breath as she watched him push himself to a seated position, back against the cliff. Moving carefully, he worked the rope beneath his arms and around his torso. When it was knotted, he looked up. His gaze met with hers, then with William's.

"I'm ready," he called.

William returned to the horse and the rope began to slide once again over the edge. Both of Isaiah's hands clasped the rope above his head as he was dragged along the cliffside. More rocks fell away, the sound of them seeming to explode in her head. Perhaps that was what pulled her from inertia. She jumped to her feet, took hold of the rope with her left hand, and added her own strength—small though it might be—to the effort. Every step she took backward brought Isaiah that much closer to safety.

Keep him safe, God. Please, keep him safe.

And at last, her prayer was answered. He was pulled over the edge, his buckskin jacket covered in dirt and torn in several places.

"Isaiah," she whispered as she went to take his arm and drag him a few more inches away from the edge.

He grimaced, his jaw clenched. "Your turn to rescue me, Miss Whitcombe."

"This was my fault."

"I doubt that." He closed his eyes.

William joined Amanda by Isaiah's side, and sounds behind them announced the arrival of the others.

Chapter Fourteen

U pon their return to the ranch, Isaiah's things were moved from the bunkhouse into what William called the guest cottage. Isaiah objected to any special treatment, but William and Amanda paid him no heed.

Oxford Grant, the physician from Gibeon, confirmed Isaiah's self-diagnosis. His left ankle had been broken when he slammed down onto the ledge. Thanks to his snug-fitting boot at the time of the break, the ankle should heal well, according to the doctor. After the bones were manipulated into their proper place—a painful experience Isaiah didn't care to repeat—his foot, ankle, and calf were wrapped in bandages stiffened with plaster of Paris.

"Stay off it," the doctor warned him. "I mean it. Bed rest and when you must be up, use crutches and don't put weight on that foot for at least the next couple of weeks. Not if you want to live without a limp."

Details of what caused Amanda's tumble over the

mountainside were repeated in Isaiah's hearing several times over the days immediately following the accident. How William had discovered the tracks of the rustlers. The mountain lion's warning cry, a sound that could make even the bravest man's blood run cold. Amanda's terrified horse and her tumble over the cliff's edge. And finally, Isaiah's rescue only to be injured himself.

"It's God's mercy either one of you are alive," Reverend Blankenship said when he heard the story as he sat in the guest cottage beside the bed.

Isaiah nodded his agreement.

"Would you care for more tea, reverend?" Amanda rose from the chair in the corner of the room, and judging by the tremor in her voice, Isaiah feared the retelling of her story had caused her anxiety.

"No, thank you." The pastor stood as well, holding the brim of his black hat between his hands. "No, I shall go and leave the patient to his rest."

Amanda led the way out of the bedroom. A moment later, Isaiah heard the front door of the cottage closing.

Rest. The last thing he needed was more rest. The skin beneath the rigid bandages itched like the dickens, but it was the itch to be up and doing something that made him wonder if he might go insane before his forced captivity was over.

Through the window, he saw Amanda talking to the reverend as he climbed into his buggy. A short while later, the rig moved out of sight. Amanda glanced toward the cottage, as if contemplating a return. Then, with a shake of her head, she walked to the main house instead.

Isaiah released a breath. He was able to admit to enjoying her concern four days ago. But he'd come to hate that she thought of him as an invalid. He wasn't. He'd broken a bone. That was all. Broken bones mended. Otherwise he was as healthy and strong as ever.

Needing to prove it, he decided to get outside for a while. He wasn't a fool. He would avoid stepping down on his left foot. He would use the crutches that leaned against the wall. But he needed to get out of this small space, even if only for a short while.

He shrugged out of his nightshirt and took the trousers he'd worn on the day of the accident from the foot of the bed. They were clean now, free of any traces of that day except for the missing left pant leg. It had been cut off at the knee by the doctor himself. With some careful maneuvering, he got dressed, including his right boot, then grabbed the crutches and rose from the bed.

Once he was outside in the light of mid-afternoon, he stopped and tipped his head back, eyes closed. It seemed longer than four days since he'd felt the sun on his face.

"Mr. Coltrane! What are you doing?"

He drew in a breath as he opened his eyes and looked toward the house. Amanda hurried toward him, a worried expression doing nothing to diminish how pretty she looked.

"I liked it better when you called me Isaiah."

"When I . . . I did no such thing." She came to a stop before him.

"You did. When you held me by the arm and pulled me away from the ridge."

"Well, I . . . Well, you . . ." She allowed the words to fade into silence, no doubt remembering the moment.

"Isaiah." He heard it echo in his memory. She'd whispered his name on that day, but it had seemed more profound than that. It had changed something within him in a way he had yet to understand. Of course, this might all have to do more with pain, restless nights, required healing, and the itch of cabin fever.

As if wanting to cause him to question his sanity even more, he heard a familiar voice shout, "Isaiah Coltrane, you old horse thief."

Steadying himself with the crutches, he turned his head away from Amanda and watched Paddy Muldoon ride into the barnyard, leading a pack mule behind his horse. "Paddy?"

"You're darn tootin' it's me." Paddy reined in, then leaned a forearm on the saddle horn. "And look at ya. All busted up."

"What are you doing here? How did you find me?"

"Weren't all that hard. You're not the only man who can follow tracks in these parts." He shrugged before dismounting. As he did so, his eyes moved from Isaiah to Amanda. "And you must be Miss Whitcombe. I see now why Isaiah was dead set on seeing you safely home." He gave her a broad wink. "I'd've wanted to do it myself if I'd known. Name's Paddy Muldoon, ma'am, and I'm right pleased to meet ya."

"Paddy," Isaiah warned in a low voice.

The older man laughed.

"How did you find me?" he asked again.

Paddy touched his temple with an index finger. "I wanted to know if you made it through the Mary Mountain and to the Overstreet ranch, so I made inquiries. Come to find out you got yourself laid up, so I packed your belongings on my mule and came down straight away to see for myself. Didn't know how bad you was or how long you'd be stayin'." He jerked his head toward the pack mule. "Tell me where to put everything, and I'll unload my mule."

It was Amanda who answered. "If you'll follow me, sir, I'll show you Mr. Coltrane's quarters."

Dumbfounded, Isaiah watched the two of them walk toward the guest cottage, Paddy leading the mule behind him.

———

HALFWAY TO THE COTTAGE, Amanda said, "Is the pinto your horse, Mr. Muldoon?"

"He is. Good little horse."

"I'm grateful for your generosity in lending him to us. I assure you, Mr. Coltrane would have returned him to you as soon as possible. He is not a horse thief."

"I knowed that. I was joshin' him, is all. That's just the way it is between us."

For some reason, it pleased Amanda to know it was that way for Isaiah with this man. Perhaps it was the mischief she saw in Paddy's eyes, but she liked the idea of him teasing Isaiah.

She took the last few steps to the cottage. "This is

where Mr. Coltrane is staying while he recovers." She lifted the latch.

"Busted his ankle. Is that what I understand?"

"Yes."

Paddy clucked his tongue. "Fool thing to do."

She stiffened, insulted on Isaiah's behalf. "He was rescuing me from a fall. I was thrown from my horse and went over a cliff."

"Ain't that how the two of you met? You fallin' off a horse."

Perhaps his teasing wasn't always likable.

"Pardon, miss. I shouldn't've said it like that."

Her ill-humor evaporated as quickly as it had come. "It's all right, Mr. Muldoon. You are entirely correct. I was thrown off a horse in Yellowstone and again earlier this week. And both times it was Mr. Coltrane who rescued me."

"Well, all I can say is, I'm glad he was around to do the rescuin'. Not surprised neither. He's that kind of man. But you might want to think again before you go gettin' on a horse." He winked a second time.

She let herself smile, desperately wishing to ask him more questions about Isaiah Coltrane. Unfortunately, the man in question arrived at that moment, swinging forward on his crutches.

Paddy ducked into the small parlor of the cottage and looked around. "Nice. Real nice." With a nod, he stepped outside again and went to the mule.

"What did you bring?" Isaiah asked, irritation in his voice.

"Pretty much everything."

Unsure what "everything" meant, Amanda moved to stand near Paddy. "Allow me to help."

"Won't say no to a pretty lady." He pulled leather saddlebags from the mule. "If it's not too heavy. It holds books. Isaiah does love his books."

The saddlebags were heavy, but not too heavy for her to carry. Curiosity made her want to empty the bags on the table inside the door. How could she not want to know what sort of books he liked to read? But she resisted the urge and took the saddlebags unopened into the bedroom where she left them on a chair.

"You shouldn't have done this, Paddy," she heard Isaiah say as she returned to the parlor.

"'Course I shoulda done it. Winter's comin' up in the mountains. You might be walkin' on that ankle in six weeks or so, but you'll still have healing to do. Broken bones tend to ache in the cold weather, and yours ain't strong. Won't be right away. Overstreet's got a good reputation. Keep workin' for him until you're back to yourself."

Oh, how she wanted to join in that conversation. How she wanted to encourage Isaiah to stay more than a few weeks. Stay through the winter. Stay until she and Roger returned to England.

She worried her lower lip. Why did it feel so important to her that he remain on Eden's Gate for the winter? Yes, she liked him. He'd rescued her. Not just once but twice. How could she not like him? And yet it felt like something more. Which, of course, it couldn't be. She didn't really know the man. She might never truly know him.

Drawing a breath, she moved toward the door, but Paddy entered the parlor before she reached it, his arms laden with bags holding heaven-only-knew what. He gave her a nod, then carried his burden to the sofa. She observed for a moment before slipping outside.

Isaiah remained where she'd last seen him, leaning on his crutches, his expression bemused. "I don't know what got into Paddy," he said. "He shouldn't have done this."

"You're mistaken, Mr. Coltrane. It is good for you to have your things around you. Perhaps having your books will make your recovery seem to go more quickly." Again, she wished she could see the contents of those saddlebags.

"I doubt that."

Odd, how his reply felt like a personal rejection.

Drawing herself up, she said, "I shall ask Mr. Kincaid to prepare something for Mr. Muldoon to eat and see that he has a place to sleep for as long as he is with us." With a small toss of her head, she strode away, telling herself she didn't care a fig what Isaiah Coltrane wanted or didn't want.

But, of course, she knew that was a lie.

Chapter Fifteen

Two mornings later, Paddy Muldoon rode out of the Overstreet barnyard at the same time that William, Amanda, Roger, and Mrs. Adler started the team of horses and surrey toward Gibeon to attend the Sunday service. A few cowboys followed the surrey, as they had the previous week. Other cowboys rode out to tend the cattle on the range.

Isaiah observed the departures and told himself he was glad to have peace and quiet all around. Only it didn't feel like peace and quiet. He felt isolated, as if he'd been deserted. A ridiculous notion. He'd spent weeks—even months—shut up in his cabin with snow piled high, making it hard to get back and forth to the small barn, let alone go anywhere else. He'd gone a couple of months and more without talking to another human being. He was used to silence. He was content to spend days with his dog and his horse.

With a huff, he returned to the bedroom in the guest

cottage and dropped onto the side of the bed. Bandit chose to sit inside the doorway.

"Some sympathy might be in order," Isaiah groused.

With a groan, Bandit lay down, nose resting on crossed paws, eyes watchful.

"You're right. I could put this time to better use."

With the aid of his crutches, he rose again, this time going to the small desk beneath the window. On it, he'd arranged all the books and journals Paddy had brought down from Montana.

"What was he thinking?"

He knew the answer to that question. Paddy hadn't wanted him to have any reason to rush back to the cabin before hard winter set in. His old friend might be a bit of a recluse himself, but he'd always been dead set against Isaiah spending his life the same way.

"You're a young man," Paddy liked to say. "You oughta live like one."

Isaiah hated to admit that the man could be right. But the truth was, he'd enjoyed his time on Eden's Gate, his broken ankle notwithstanding. It had been pleasant working with William and the other cowboys. In fact, it frustrated him that he hadn't been able to complete the job of finding the rustlers. Other men were out there now, doing what he'd wanted to be doing.

Amanda's image walked in his mind, and he was forced to admit that it wasn't just William and his ranch hands who'd made his stay pleasurable. He rather liked it when Amanda brought the meals to the cottage. He rather liked the times she lingered with questions about his life in Montana or answered his questions about her life in England. When he lived in the East, he'd preferred to avoid young women of wealth and privilege. The ones he'd known had never seemed to have much going on in their heads beyond new gowns and potential marriages. The same could not be said of Amanda Whitcombe.

He gave his head a slow shake as he settled on the chair at the desk. He reached for the first of the journals and thumbed through the pages. It contained the stories of Josiah Anderson, a true mountain man.

His thoughts drifted back to the many evenings he'd spent with the old trapper, recording Josiah's experiences from another time and place into this journal. Josiah had been in his late eighties by then while Isaiah had been a boy of seventeen, held captive by the tales of the west, before the buffalo had been killed in mass numbers, before the beavers had been trapped until they were rare, until wagon trains had carried thousands of hopeful families to new lives in Oregon and California, until the iron horse had joined east coast and west coast of this great nation.

Even as he grew frail with age, Josiah had spent his last years encouraging men in government to do more to protect nature, to rescue the buffalo, to promote conservation in the land that he loved. And when Josiah passed away, Isaiah had mourned the old mountain man as deeply as he later mourned the passing of his own father.

He ran his finger over the spines of the other journals, journals filled with the stories of men who had experienced the adventures that came with exploring new lands, discovering new passes through the mountains, meeting new people groups. From the moment Isaiah started his own journey west in 1886, he'd made it a point of recording the stories he heard along the way from those who had been there before him, including stories from men of the Shoshone, Cheyenne, and Crow tribes. The results of all that writing—more than ten years of it—were arranged on the desk before him.

He slipped the first journal back into its place, then pulled the latest one from the others and opened it to the first blank page. He hadn't made many entries in recent weeks, and only a single one since meeting Amanda. Not for lack of trying. But every time he held his pencil between his fingers, he felt the inadequacy of his own words. All he wanted to write about was her, but he felt unable to do her justice, even when there was so much to tell. Amanda being swept down river. Amanda seated by a campfire, wet and cold. Amanda challenging him with that determined tilt of her chin. Amanda's eyes filled with tears. Amanda laughing. Amanda clinging to a narrow ledge, frightened and brave at the same time.

Paddy's voice taunted him. *"You sweet on her?"*

He picked up his pencil and tried again.

AMANDA FELT A QUICKENING of her pulse as the surrey came over a rise and the house at Eden's Gate came into view. All through the church service, she'd wondered how Isaiah was getting along. His friend had left that morning, and everyone else had scattered to the wind. Perhaps he shouldn't have been left alone for such a long time. Of course, he was mobile on his crutches, and he could do most anything he needed to do without any help from her or anyone else. Still—

"Amanda?" William said softly beside her.

"Hmm?"

"Would you be able to spare me a few minutes in my study when we get back to the ranch?"

Only half-listening—her thoughts on Isaiah and not William—she answered. "If you wish."

"I wish."

She couldn't see the cottage. It was on the other side of the main house, but she knew precisely what it looked like at midday, sunlight warming its silver-stoned exterior. She'd always thought it a wonderful addition to the collection of outbuildings and corrals and paddocks of Eden's Gate. It would even look quite lovely tucked into the woods at Hooke Manor.

Of course, she could ask Sebastian to have a replica built, but it would never be the same, even if it did look lovely in that setting. Because it—and everything on Eden's Gate—belonged in this place, here in Idaho with those majestic mountains rising in the east. She drew in a deep breath as she stared at the Teton range. How she would miss this view when she had to return to England.

A short while later, the surrey pulled into the barnyard. Amanda's gaze darted toward the cottage, but there was no sign of Isaiah coming out to meet them.

William disembarked, then assisted her to the ground. Instead of releasing her hand immediately, he tucked it into the crook of his arm and escorted her toward the front door. It took a moment for her to remember his request for a few minutes in his study. Now she wondered if she should be concerned. Had he received some kind of bad news? Was Sebastian all right? Jocelyn? What could he wish to discuss with her? Especially in his study rather than at the table over a meal? This seemed so formal. William Overstreet was not a formal type of man. But neither did he appear upset or tense. Their siblings, now married to each other, must be well.

Delicious odors filled the house, announcing that Sunday dinner was not far off. Her stomach threatened to growl as they walked past the parlor, down a short hallway, and into William's office. The first time she'd seen this room, it had been in utter disarray, the shambles at least partially blamed upon William's serious injury, incurred in an encounter with an American buffalo. But Sebastian had assisted Jocelyn in getting everything back in order, and much to Amanda's surprise, the office had remained that way even after the earl and his bride departed Eden's Gate.

"Go ahead." He closed the door behind them. "Say it."

She raised her eyebrows in question.

He chuckled. "You're surprised to see it's still organized."

"Perhaps a *little* surprised." She settled onto a chair and waited while he rounded the large desk to take his own seat. It was when he steepled his fingers in front of his chin that a sense of dread returned. He looked all too much like her brother.

"Amanda, I am concerned."

"Stop, William. Please."

He cocked an eyebrow as he tapped his chin with his index fingers.

"Don't try to be Sebastian."

"I'm not trying to be him."

"But you are. I can see it in your eyes." She motioned at him. "In your posture. In the way you're holding your hands."

He straightened in his chair, at the same time lowering his hands. "Amanda, you know how reluctant Sebastian was to leave you at Eden's Gate when he and Jocelyn went to England. You may have worn him down, but I had to promise him that I would look out for you. I made a solemn oath. But considering what happened to you in the park and then again last week, I haven't done a very good job of keeping that promise. You might have been killed. Either time."

"But I wasn't killed. I wasn't even seriously injured."

"You might have been," he repeated as he leaned toward her.

She leaned forward too. "But I *wasn't.*"

With an exasperated breath, he pulled back. "Sebastian is one of the best friends I've ever had."

"And he's my brother and I love him dearly."

"Then we are agreed that we need to take better care of you."

"Better care?"

"No more chasing rustlers."

She nodded. "I daresay that is not unreasonable."

"I would prefer it if you stayed closer to the ranch house in the months to come."

"Noted."

He eyed her for a long while in silence before saying, "Noted but not agreed?"

She gave him her sweetest smile, the one that had always worked on both Father and Sebastian.

He laughed.

"Is that everything?" She prepared to rise.

His smile vanished. "No. There is one more thing."

She settled back onto the chair.

"It's about Mr. Coltrane."

"Mr. Col—?" Her heart raced. "Has something happened to Isaiah?" She wanted to run from the room, but William's gaze kept her frozen in place.

"No, Amanda. My concern is you."

"Whatever do you mean?"

"I'm speaking of your . . . growing attraction for the man."

"My growing—" She broke off again, unable to come up with a suitable response. Because, of course, he spoke the truth. She was undeniably attracted to Isaiah. Even surprise that William had discerned her affection wouldn't allow her to deny it.

He steepled his hands once again. "I like Mr. Coltrane. I have heard nothing but good about him. He's an excellent tracker. He's honest and he's God-fearing. But you are Lady Amanda Whitcombe. You are the daughter of an earl and now the sister of an earl. Your family name is held in high regard throughout England. There are great expectations for you when it comes to marriage."

"William, stop!"

"I don't want to see you get your heart broken because of a man you could never marry."

She shot to her feet. "You have no right to say such things to me, William Overstreet. And who are you to say who I could or could not marry? Your sister ran a shipping concern and my brother thought her very suitable to become his wife. So did Father—at the end."

"The Overstreets may be in trade, Amanda, but that is something quite different from Mr. Coltrane."

"Why? Because they were wealthy enough to send their eldest son to England for an education? There are some things more important in a husband than how much money he has or where he ranks in society."

"Amanda, please sit down." He spoke softly but there was determination in his tone.

"All right." She sank back onto the chair. "Say what you must."

He drew in a slow breath. "If you allow this infatuation to continue, please explain to me where it could lead. Would you want to take Mr. Coltrane with you to England? That is, if he would even be willing."

She frowned, her gaze lowered to her hands in her lap. She could not imagine Isaiah seated in the drawing room at Hooke Manor or at the large dining table during one of the elaborate Whitcombe banquets. He wasn't uneducated or uncouth, so that wasn't the reason. In fact, he was well-spoken and intelligent. She simply knew, deep in her soul, that he would not want to be there, that he would be like a caged wild animal in a city zoo.

Meeting William's gaze, she said, "I will give it some thought." She stood and walked to the door. "And if you don't mind, I believe I'll eat dinner in my room."

Chapter Sixteen

A couple of hours later, a rap sounded on Amanda's bedroom door. Assuming it was Mrs. Adler, come to take the tray away, she called, "Yes?"

The door eased open, and Roger's head poked into view. "It is I."

"Come in, Roger."

He did so, leaving the door ajar behind him. "Are you unwell?"

"No." She gave him a half-hearted smile. "But you already know that, do you not?"

He returned the smile, his more genuine than hers. "Yes."

"You and William must have discussed me over Sunday dinner."

"We did." He sat on the chair near the window. "What else could we discuss, just the two of us at table? As much as I like William, we have absolutely nothing in common other than you and your brother. And so you and Sebastian are what we talk about."

"Do you agree with William?"

"That isn't the most important question, Amanda."

"No." She released a sigh as she rose and walked to the window. Several of the ranch hands sat on the ground conversing in the shade of tall trees near the corner of the house. The leaves were still green, but it would not be long before they began to turn colors. "William asked me where my feelings for Isaiah could lead. That's what I must know. Isn't it?"

"I would say so."

She faced him. "But *I* am the one who must know. Not others."

Roger leaned forward, elbows on knees, his hands clasped. "Amanda, your brother is my dearest friend. We are not of the same class. I am the son of a shop-keeper. Quite a successful one, but society has never considered me fit company for a viscount or an earl. But my friendship with him developed and endured despite my humble background. Then there is William. He's an American. That was even worse than being the son of a shopkeeper in your father's eyes. And yet Sebastian's friendship never wavered from William either. And look at Sebastian with Adam. He could have shunned your half-brother because of the circumstances of his birth. Instead, he loves and respects him. He never excludes him. Sebastian is unafraid to let others know how he feels about Adam, and others are more respectful of Adam because of it."

Amanda felt her heart lighten with hope.

"But Sebastian is a man," Roger continued. "And whether you like it or not, society will always allow a man, especially one who is now an earl, the discretion to do things, to make certain choices, that it will never allow the gentler sex. That it will never allow you."

"That is ever so unfair."

"Quite so. It isn't fair. But it is true."

Amanda sat again and covered her face with her hands. "I cannot help what I feel."

"My dear girl, you have always been a fascinating combination of society hostess and puckish spirit, like something out of one of Shakespeare's own plays. There's a wildness in you—untamed, free, full of laughter—that no ballroom could ever contain."

She lowered her hands to look at him.

"But society . . . well, society can be terribly unforgiving. A man like Isaiah Coltrane is hardly the sort of match people will expect for you. If you were to marry him, there would be whispers, raised eyebrows, and no shortage of opinions. Society clings to its rules—rules that are much less kind to those who dare step outside of them." He shook his head. "I dare say, would that bring happiness to either of you?"

"Roger, I don't even know if he likes me. Not in that way. He is polite and friendly, but nothing more. Why must you and William both warn me away from him? Could I not be his friend, the way I am your friend, the way I am William's?"

He leaned back on the chair, studying her. "Perhaps you could. But if that is all you want, why are you so upset by our warnings?"

She didn't know how to answer him. It was confusing. She felt something strong for Isaiah. There was no doubting that. The thought of him leaving Eden's Gate once his ankle healed or of her returning to England while knowing she would never see him again made her chest ache. But that didn't mean she wanted to spend her life with him. Did it? She hadn't thought of marriage. Had she?

"If you allow this infatuation to continue, please explain to me where it could lead. Would you want to take Mr. Coltrane with you to England?"

While William's words replayed in her memory, Roger rose. "I'll leave you with your thoughts." He left the room, closing the door softly behind him.

———

Isaiah sat in the shade with his back against the house, listening to Logan Coe strum his guitar while singing a familiar hymn. After the first verse, Isaiah joined in with the others seated on the ground or leaning against trees.

"'Just as I am, and waiting not / To rid my soul of one dark blot, / To Thee, whose blood can cleanse each spot, / O Lamb of God, I come, I come.'"

While Isaiah often sang a familiar hymn while alone in the forest, he had to admit there was something special about raising his voice in praise along with other believers.

"'Just as I am, though tossed about / With many a conflict, many a doubt, / Fightings and fears within, without, / O Lamb of God, I come, I come.'"

Above the singing, Isaiah heard the hard closing of a door. Soon after, Amanda strode into view on her way to the barn. She didn't look toward the trees where the cowboys were gathered on a quiet Sunday afternoon. Was she even aware they were there? Surely she heard their singing.

"'Just as I am, Thou wilt receive, / Wilt welcome, pardon, cleanse, relieve; / Because Thy promise I believe, / O Lamb of God, I come, I come.'"

He reached for the crutches and stood on his good foot while adjusting the crutches under his arms. Then, with a nod of apology in Logan's direction, he started toward the barn. He found Amanda near the entrance, her Palouse mare tied to a rail while she brushed the horse's black and white coat. They'd spent little time in each other's company in the days since he'd returned to the ranch with a broken ankle. Too little if Isaiah were honest with himself. He'd grown somewhat nostalgic for his time alone with her in Yellowstone.

"Going for a ride?"

She gasped and jumped back a step. Only then did he realize she hadn't heard his approach.

"Sorry," he said.

With a nod, she resumed grooming the mare, her gaze on the horse and not him.

"Is something wrong, Miss Whitcombe?"

"No."

It was tempting to say he didn't believe her, but he didn't suppose that would improve her agitated mood. He cleared his throat. "How was church?"

"Quite lovely. As always."

"The boys were singing some hymns just now."

"Yes. I heard them."

Had their conversations been this stilted when she had a knot on her head and couldn't remember her own name? He didn't think so.

"Well, I guess I'll leave you to it." He prepared to swivel around on his crutches.

"Isaiah?"

He hid a smile, loving the sound of his Christian name on her lips.

"Would you . . . Have you ever wanted to see England? Or Europe?"

He frowned. He hadn't known what she meant to ask, but it certainly wasn't that. Still, his answer came quickly. "I've never given much thought to traveling abroad. Couldn't afford it now, of course, but my interest, ever since I was a boy, was always the American West, not the old lands on the other side of the Atlantic."

"I understand. I truly do. When Father took us to see Buffalo Bill's Wild West in London, I was frightfully taken by it all. The rescuing of passengers in the runaway stagecoach. The trick riders. The sharpshooters. And the horses, of course. I fell in love with the Palouse horses." She ran the brush along Ebony's spine from mane to tail, as if to prove her point. "From that moment on, I wanted to come to America to see this land for myself."

"Bill Cody knows how to put on a show. There's no denying that. But much of it is just that. A show. The reality can be quite different, and much of what was once real is gone now."

"But not everything."

"No. Not everything." Steadying himself with his crutches, he looked over his shoulder toward the Tetons, the rocky mountaintops bathed in sunlight. "Some things will always remain."

Amanda left her horse and came to stand beside him. "It's ever so beautiful." She spoke softly, reverence in her voice.

Isaiah wished he could drop a crutch and put an arm around her shoulders.

"I'm glad I got to see it for myself."

He looked down at her. "I'm glad you did too."

She met his gaze, eyes serious. "Do you ever imagine leaving the West?"

"No." He shook his head, offering a small smile. "I don't ever imagine it. This is where I belong. It's home."

"I wish I was as certain about my future." She looked in the direction of the mountains again. "Others think they know what my future should be, but I'm not at all sure I want what they want for me."

He recalled his first impressions of her. Spoiled. Haughty. Entitled. None of those attributes had turned out to be true. Oh, certainly she was used to the finer things in life, but she didn't seem to require them. She didn't expect them as her due.

"And this will always be your home," she added.

Yes, this would always be his home. But he wondered if she would ever consider staying and making it her home too.

Chapter Seventeen

S everal days later, late in the day, Isaiah was making his way from the cottage to the bunkhouse when three men rode into the barnyard, stirring up a cloud of dust as they reined to a halt. He recognized Frank Lewis, the sheriff from Gibeon, in the lead.

Frank tipped his head in Isaiah's direction before dismounting. By that time, William was striding out of the house.

"What is it?" William asked without delay.

"Good news. They tracked the rustlers to a hideout up in Montana." He looked toward Isaiah again. "Just like Mr. Coltrane suspected." He returned his gaze to William. "Most of the rustlers were captured. A couple got away. Another one of them was shot and died. The posse wasn't able to recover all the cattle. The ones stolen earlier in the summer were already long gone. Sold at market. But these latest thefts, those cattle are on their way back to Idaho even now."

William grinned. "That is good news. Great news."

Isaiah looked down at his broken ankle and wanted to curse it. If not for that stupid fall, if not for hitting that ledge so hard and snapping a bone, he could have been in on the apprehension of the thieves. Maybe he could have gone after the two who got away, making sure none of them were free to steal again. He'd already resented the forced inactivity, but he felt it ever more keenly now, knowing what he'd missed.

When he looked up again, Amanda stood at William's side. As she was told the news, she smiled in his direction, and suddenly he didn't resent the need to stay at Eden's Gate instead of hunting down cattle thieves. At least not as much as he had before.

KNOWING the cattle thieves wouldn't plague the valley again brightened the mood of everyone on the ranch, and Amanda was delighted when William announced he would host a barbecue and barn dance on the following Saturday. All the ranchers who lived south of Eden's Gate, along with their hired hands, would be invited. So would the townsfolk in Gibeon.

"What can I do to help?" she asked the housekeeper as soon as she heard of the party plans.

"Not sure you should help. You're a paid guest, remember."

"When have I not wanted to fully participate, Mrs. Adler? You shouldn't treat me any differently than you treated Jocelyn when she was here."

A wistful expression flashed across the woman's face—no doubt because she missed Jocelyn, the new Countess of Hooke—but the sentiment wasn't allowed to remain. Mrs. Adler crossed her arms beneath her ample bosom. "As you wish, Miss Amanda. If we're going to play host to the entire valley in three days time, we're going to need every dish, plate, pot, and pan this ranch owns. Let's you and me get started with some cleaning and organizing." She turned on a heel and headed for the dining room.

Amanda wondered what could possibly be left to clean or organize since those tasks were Mrs. Adler's speciality. She ran the Eden's Gate household with the same precision as the Hooke Manor butler ran his domain. But Amanda didn't have to think long about what to do next. The housekeeper put her to work and was always somewhere nearby with more instructions. What surprised Amanda was that she enjoyed the tasks assigned to her. It was fun to see the plans come together and to know all that went on behind the scenes to prepare for a large event. She'd served as the hostess in her father's home even before her first London season, arranging dinner parties and balls. In those years, she'd sent plenty of instructions to the housekeeper and the cook. But she'd never actually been elbow deep in the preparations as she was now.

When Mrs. Adler announced they'd accomplished enough, she looked at Amanda and added, "You're a hard worker, miss. I never would've expected it." She punctuated the compliment with a firm nod.

Amanda beamed. Silly as it might be, she liked

hearing the housekeeper's praise, especially when she remembered the woman's initial, less than welcoming reaction upon meeting the guests from England. And while Mrs. Adler had warmed to all of them over the summer, this felt even better.

"What will we do tomorrow?"

Mrs. Adler smiled. "I'll have a word with Mr. William after dinner. Don't worry. There is plenty yet to be done before Saturday. I won't let you stay idle."

---

18 September 1895

Dearest Sebastian and Jocelyn,

It has been nearly two weeks since I wrote my last letter to you. Each day I hope I will receive one from you. You are both missed so much. The house does feel emptier without the two of you here.

Roger goes off most days with his paints. I rarely see him after breakfast or before supper. I am not sure how much longer he will be able to spend his days outdoors. Although they remain sunny and mostly pleasant, the nights have turned quite cold. The men mention winter more often, and I believe I see dread in some of their eyes when they mention snow.

As I wrote to you in my last letter, the rustlers hit ranchers in the valley again. But thanks to Mr. Coltrane, the game scout I mentioned before, they were tracked to a hiding place in Montana. A number of them were arrested, and the sheriff hopes the remainder will be caught and brought to justice soon. This is a just ending to the troubles that beset William and the other ranchers this summer. Mr. Coltrane was injured early in the pursuit and was not involved at the end. And I fear the fault for his injury was mine. I will tell you more about that when we are together again.

With the rustlers caught, William decided to throw a grand party this coming Saturday. As I understand it, everyone who lives within traveling distance will be present. They will barbecue beef and there will be a great amount of other food as well. Dishes prepared by Mr. Kincaid—I still find it hard to call him Chuck as you did—and many dishes prepared by those who come from town and other ranches. There will be music and dancing. I have never been to a barn dance, but I am quite sure it will be like no ball I ever attended.

Do you remember our last ball at Hooke Manor? It was such a special night for Adam and Eliza. How are they? It's been almost a month since I received a letter from Eliza.

I hope you are both settling into your new roles. While I would love to see you there and be with you as you host your first parties, I can honestly say that I am in no rush to return to England. With every passing day, this feels more and more like home to me. And the people around me feel more and more like family. I do not actually have proper words to describe the way I feel, and so I will end this letter letting you know how thankful I am that you, Sebastian, did not insist I return to England before my year is up.

Your loving sister,
Amanda

————

SINCE THE DAY Isaiah had been released from bed rest by the physician, he'd taken his meals with the ranch hands around a large table at one end of the bunkhouse. The mood on that Wednesday evening was jubilant. It was more than just the capture of the rustlers. A big party was being planned. A party with plenty of good food, music, and dancing. Not to mention single young women from around the valley. That was always a treat for the men. From the good natured ribbing Logan was taking at the moment, Isaiah suspected the youngest of the cowboys had a very specific girl he wanted to see on Saturday.

The same was true of Isaiah. Only the young woman he wanted to see lived on Eden's Gate. With a little effort, he could see her every day. But he hadn't made the effort. Not since Sunday. Because on Sunday he'd begun to want something he believed was impossible to have. A future where he wasn't alone, just him, his dog, and his horse. A future that included a woman with a warm smile and a laugh that could brighten a room and sometimes a propensity to talk too much.

"Too bad about your ankle," Jake said to Isaiah, intruding on his thoughts. "You'll miss the dancing."

Isaiah looked down at his left foot. "I never considered myself much of a dancer. Maybe it's just as well I'm kept off the dance floor. For the sake of all the ladies and their delicate feet." He wished he could add that he wouldn't mind holding Amanda in his arms for a song or two. Common sense kept him silent.

"Been a long time since we had a barn dance," Rocky said. "Coulda been one after the wedding, but folks weren't much in the mood for dancing, what with the groom's pa being so sick and all."

"What was he like?" Isaiah asked. "The earl."

Logan answered, "Right cantankerous type. At least he seemed so when he first got here. You know. Nose in the air, lookin' down on us all, barking orders. But he seemed different after a while. Not that we got to spend much time with him. His sickness didn't let him mingle much outside the family." He grinned. "But enough that it was clear he was like putty in Miss Amanda's hands."

"And her brother?"

"Sebastian?" Jake leaned his elbows on the table. "He's the one who surprised me most. He could sound highfalutin, the way he talked, but he wasn't. Right from the start, he was out with the men. Even helped us bring down a grizzly that was killing Eden's Gate cows."

Isaiah's eyes widened. "He shot a grizzly?"

"Him and Miss Jocelyn both. Fired their rifles at that charging bear. After that, I don't reckon any of us were surprised when they decided to get hitched. They seemed made for each other."

Made for each other. No one would say that about him and Amanda. They were worlds apart, no matter how well she sat a horse or how brave she was in dangerous situations or how much she loved this country he called home. And the sooner he accepted that fact, the better off he would be.

Chapter Eighteen

Amanda stared at her reflection in the mirror, nerves fluttering in her midsection as she ran her right hand over the yellow and blue fabric of her gown, one of her favorites that she'd brought from England. The sensation in her abdomen bemused her. While today might be her first barn dance, it wasn't her first large party. She'd attended many balls in the years since her debut, and she'd played hostess to countless guests at Hooke Manor. She knew how to be certain others were comfortable and having a good time. She knew how to divert a conversation when it strayed into dangerous waters. And she had an uncanny ability to know when two people would be absolutely right for one another.

As I would be right for Isaiah.

She pressed the flat of her hand against her stomach, wishing that thought hadn't popped into her head. The fluttering of her nerves had tripled because of it.

She'd barely seen Isaiah this past week. Not since Sunday afternoon when she'd prepared Ebony for a ride, still wrestling with her emotions after her talks with William and with Roger. More than once she'd wished she had some excuse to go to the guest cottage. But Isaiah wasn't an invalid. He was able to move about on his crutches at will. He took his meals with the other men in the bunkhouse. How he filled the majority of his days, she didn't know. All she knew for certain was that he didn't seek her out.

The rattle of harness and the sound of merry voices wafted through her open window, and she looked outside in time to see six wagons and buggies, as well as men on horseback, approaching on the road from Gibeon.

After a last glance in the mirror, Amanda left the bedroom. She reached the bottom of the stairs at the same moment William appeared out of his study.

"Sounds as if our guests have begun to arrive," he said.

"Yes. I saw them from my window."

He offered the crook of his arm. "Then let's go welcome them. Shall we?"

She'd tried to stay angry with William this past week, but her irritation hadn't lasted. She knew he'd spoken out of concern, unable to keep himself from trying to fill the role of elder brother.

As he pulled open the front door, he said, "By the way, you look very pretty. I predict you won't sit out a single dance once the music starts."

She laughed, enjoying the compliment, even while knowing there was only one man she wished to dance with—and he wouldn't be able to oblige because of his broken ankle. But maybe Isaiah didn't know how to dance. Or maybe he didn't like to dance. Or maybe he wouldn't want to partner with her even if he knew how or liked to.

Although Amanda had helped with preparations for today's event, she still felt some surprise upon seeing how transformed the barnyard appeared. Long tables covered in red and white tablecloths had been set up near the barn. Fire pits had been dug, and large cuts of beef roasted over them now, the meat skewered on rods or laid on grates. Metal lanterns with glass sides hung everywhere, from tree limbs, fence posts, and poles driven into the earth in strategic places. None were lit at this point, but come nightfall they would cast a golden glow over everything, both inside and outside the barn. Buggies and wagons came to a halt at this point, and men, women, and children disembarked, many of them carrying covered plates and dishes to set upon the tables.

William escorted Amanda to a central place where they could welcome people as they arrived and milled about. She played her part as hostess with ease, introducing herself to those whom she hadn't met and exchanging polite conversation with those she already knew.

They couldn't have asked for a more beautiful afternoon for the barbecue. The late September day was warm without being stifling. Sitting in the sunshine to eat would be pleasant. A good thing since there were far too many guests for the amount of shade nature and the house and barn could provide. Still, she knew she would need her shawl once the sun set.

"Miss Whitcombe," Harry Hathaway said to her, "if you don't look as pretty as the morning sun on the river."

"Why, thank you, sir."

Harry's wife, Margaret, added, "What have you heard from your brother?"

"Not a thing, Mrs. Hathaway." Amanda suspected the woman already knew there'd been no letters or telegrams from Sebastian or his bride. Margaret Hathaway ran the Teton General Store and served as the post mistress for people in Gibeon and the surrounding area.

"Well, when you write to them, give them our best. Too bad they couldn't be with us tonight. Been too long since we've had a barn dance in these parts. Going to be a fun night."

The Hathaways moved on. Next came Truman Blankenship and Oxford Grant. The reverend—a man only two or three years older than Amanda—was a bachelor. The doctor was a man in his mid-fifties and a widower. She wondered if either of them enjoyed dancing. And that question made her think of Isaiah once again.

She glanced around the gathering, at the small groups here and there engaged in conversations. She couldn't find Isaiah among any of them. Was he still in the cottage? Did he plan to attend the barbecue? She'd never had the opportunity to ask him, but surely he would be there. There was no reason for him to stay away. He could retire when the dancing started, if he chose.

Isaiah leaned a shoulder against a tree, observing people mingling about the barnyard. From where he stood he could watch William and Amanda as they greeted folks.

Amanda looked every inch the role of affluent hostess. So striking in that beautiful gown, unlike anything he'd seen her wear before. So different from the woman he'd pulled from the river in Yellowstone. If she belonged anywhere in America, she belonged on a ranch like Eden's Gate with a man of wealth and influence like William Overstreet. Not the first time that thought had crossed his mind since his arrival at the ranch.

He wanted to stride over to where they stood and position himself between them. He wanted to lay claim to her, despite knowing it was something he shouldn't want, couldn't have. Despite Amanda stating weeks ago that William was like a brother to her, an image flashed in his head of a couple of bull elk in rutting season, heads down, locking antlers, fighting over territory and harems, and it appalled him to how close to the truth of his feelings that image was.

God help him. He'd lost all perspective. He should get out of this place. He should go back to Montana before he made a complete fool of himself. A fool over a woman. A woman like Amanda Whitcombe. A British aristocrat who didn't belong in his world. Nor he in hers.

"Isaiah."

The sound of his name caused him to start. He

turned his gaze from Amanda and watched Oxford Grant walk toward him, a glass of punch in his hand.

"You look well," the doctor said.

"I am. Bored but feeling fine."

"Bored?" He glanced around the barnyard, as if wondering why someone could be bored with so much good food on the tables and so many good folks gathering together.

"I'm ready to be back to work," Isaiah added.

"Oh. That." Dr. Grant smiled and nodded. "A common complaint. But you'll be rid of those crutches soon. That will allow you to do more, although I advise against doing too much until the bones have time to knit back together more thoroughly."

"I'll be careful." He had to be careful. He had to heal up and leave before snow began to fall.

The doctor gave him a pat on the shoulder. "Good to know." Then, with a nod, he moved on.

Isaiah's gaze returned to where William and Amanda had stood moments before. Only Amanda was no longer with the host. His heart skipped a beat, then sped up, as he looked for her. He found her engaged in conversation with a couple of young women who appeared to be close to her age. He thought he recognized one of them—the redhead—from the church in Gibeon, even though he'd only had an opportunity to attend one Sunday service before being injured.

Amanda laughed at something, her head tipped slightly back. The sight of her enjoying herself made him smile too. And somehow he found himself with the crutches under his arms, swinging his way toward her. Despite all the reasons he shouldn't. He'd closed half the distance when she turned her head and saw his approach. The smile slipped away from her lips, and he stopped moving, his breath catching. But then her smile returned, even brighter than before.

"Mr. Coltrane, join us." She motioned him forward with a hand.

He came. He couldn't have done otherwise.

"Mr. Coltrane, I'd like you to meet Miss Bertha Hathaway and Miss Wynona Peterman."

Balancing the crutch beneath his armpit, Isaiah raised his right hand to touch the brim of his hat. "Pleasure to meet you both."

"Mr. Coltrane," they responded in unison.

"Mr. Coltrane works for Mr. Overstreet. In fact, it was he who helped William and the others find where the rustlers had driven the stolen cattle."

Bertha responded, "Then we have you to thank for this barbecue and barn dance." She punctuated her words with a laugh that somehow matched her curly red hair and the freckles splashed across her cheeks and nose.

He shook his head. "I don't think so, Miss Hathaway. That was all William's doing."

"Were you injured when you took down the rustlers?" Wynona asked.

"No." His gaze flicked to Amanda and back. "I broke my ankle before the thieves were caught. I wasn't with the posse in Montana."

"All the same," Wynona said, her head tilted slightly

to one side as she looked up at him through thick lashes, "I'm sure you were very brave."

Thankfully, before he had to decide how to reply, the dinner gong clanged, a sound that carried above the din of conversations.

William stood on the steps near the back door of the house. "Friends. Neighbors. Welcome to Eden's Gate." All eyes turned in his direction. "We've got plenty to be thankful for today. God willing, we won't be troubled by rustlers again. So let's say a word of thanks to the Lord Almighty so we can dig into all the great food laid out for us." He motioned toward the tables.

The air quieted even more, and William said a brief but meaningful prayer. The moment he said, "Amen," people began talking again.

Amanda stepped close to Isaiah, almost as if putting herself between him and the other two women. "Why don't you find a place to sit, Mr. Coltrane, and I'll bring you a plate. It would be difficult to manage that with those crutches." She glanced at Bertha and Wynona. "Excuse us."

Isaiah managed not to grin, loving that she'd laid claim to him—unwittingly perhaps—for this one afternoon. He intended to enjoy every moment of it.

Chapter Nineteen

There was a bench near the door of the guest cottage that was the perfect size for two people. It was also well away from where other guests had gathered to eat, some at tables, some on benches and chairs scattered beneath the trees and near the east wall of the house.

Isaiah settled onto the bench and laid his crutches on the ground nearby. Long shadows had begun to spread across the barnyard as the sun fell lower in the western sky. He wondered if Roger Bernhardt longed to get his paints or sketchbook in order to capture the scene. Even with so many people present, there was a peacefulness about it that warmed him.

Isaiah had never mingled with many of the residents of Gardiner. His cabin in Montana was nearly a two-hour ride from town, even when conditions were good. In the winter, he was often snowed in. In the summer, he was mostly working in Yellowstone. But he could see—watching the guests and ranch hands milling about, filling their plates, finding places to sit and eat and visit —that it might be good to be part of a community like this one. Folks caring about folks. God had created people to be social beings.

Amanda appeared through the crowd carrying two plates. The fabric of her gown—the colors of sunshine and a summer sky—swished a little as she walked. He heard it even above the din of conversations. Or maybe he only thought he heard it because of the way it swayed as she moved toward him.

She smiled as she handed him a plate overflowing with food—slices of roast beef, cornbread smothered with butter, beans baked in brown sugar, potato salad with chunks of boiled eggs, green beans with bits of bacon. Once he'd balanced the plate on his knees, she gave him a knife and fork. "There wasn't room on the plate for every choice, but I should have asked if there was something you don't like to eat."

"I'm good with whatever's set before me."

"There would have been room for us at one of the tables. It might be easier to eat there."

He pictured her seated on the ground near a campfire, the way he'd seen her so often in the park. She wasn't afraid to rough it. He knew that for a fact. But she hadn't worn a beautiful gown then. She hadn't looked like the grand lady she was in real life.

"Is something troubling you?" she asked.

"We can move to the table if you'd rather."

"No." Her gaze went to the crowd of people across the barnyard from them. "No, I like it better here. We can talk more freely."

"I'd hate it if you ruined that gown you're wearing."

"I won't. I'm quite agile, you know. I can balance a plate while I eat."

He frowned. "But you shouldn't have to."

"I don't have to. I want to."

He turned his head to meet her gaze. A man could drown in those eyes. At least, he could. And a man would do just about anything to earn one of her smiles. At least, he would.

"Mr. Coltrane?"

"Yes?"

"Are you aware that I . . . I care for you?"

His mouth went dry. He forgot the food on the plate.

"That's terribly bold of me, I know. My father would be horrified that I would dare declare my feelings before a man had done so first. But I . . . I need you to know how I feel."

"Miss Whitcombe—"

"Please call me Amanda."

"Miss Whitcombe—"

More softly, "Please."

He was powerless against her in that moment. "Amanda."

A small smile curved the corners of her mouth.

"I would never want to hurt you, Amanda."

"How would you hurt me?" she asked, still smiling.

"Because I can never be the kind of man you deserve."

"What sort of man is that?"

"A man of position and wealth, I would think. I'm

sure there are plenty of them lining up back in England, ready to court you and win your affections."

"I have been courted by such men, Mr. Coltrane." She took a breath. "Isaiah."

His heart seemed to jump at her use, once again, of his given name.

"I have been courted by such men, and none have won my affections."

"That could change."

The smile slipped away. "But it won't change. Not now that I know you."

"Your brother would never sanction . . . anything serious between us." He looked toward the crowd of people opposite them. "Neither would William."

"Forget others, Isaiah. What do *you* think?"

"I think—" He cleared his throat. "I think there are many reasons it would not be wise to allow . . . to allow ourselves to feel anything for the other beyond friendship."

"Yes, there are many reasons. But do they matter?"

Did he hear a touch of humor in her response? No, that couldn't be. There was nothing to laugh about in this situation. Nothing.

He cleared his throat a second time. "I am no one of importance, Amanda. I have little to offer a woman, any woman, and so I have never intended to offer what little I have. That gown you're wearing? It probably cost more than what I earned in the last year. Perhaps the last two years."

"I do not need this gown or any others like it."

"Perhaps you don't need it, but you would miss it if you could never have another."

"You don't know that." There was no humor in her voice now.

"I do know it."

She rose from the bench abruptly. It amazed him that she didn't spill her entire plate down the front of the gown that had become the object of their discussion. She faced him, flint in her eyes. The same eyes he'd found himself drowning in not so long ago. "Isaiah Coltrane, you obviously do not know me the way you think you do or you wouldn't say such a thing." Her voice was soft, not carrying to others, but there was steel in it, all the same. "I know my own mind and I know my own heart. I have no desire to go back to England. I want to remain in America. I don't want ballrooms. I want friends gathered in a barnyard in the shadow of the Rocky Mountains. You say you will never be the type of man I deserve, a man of position and wealth. And I tell you I don't want a man of position and wealth. I want a man of integrity. I want a man who faces danger and does not shrink from it. I want a man who steps in where he is needed. I want a man who stands on a mountain trail on a foggy Sunday morning and quotes Scripture in praise to God."

Isaiah blinked, left speechless.

With a small toss of her head, she twirled around with another swish of her skirts and walked away, leaving him alone with an overflowing plate.

Two hours later, with lanterns lit and lively music playing, Amanda spun around the interior of the barn in the arms of a cowboy whose name she'd forgotten. When the song ended, she was quite happy to be escorted to a corner where she could sit and catch her breath.

But the moment she sat on the chair against the wall, she wondered where Isaiah was. Was he watching the dancing? Did it bother him to know she was having a wonderful time despite his rejection of her? Was he pondering what she'd said to him?

The musicians—playing violin, banjo, guitar, and harmonica—started up another song, and couples took to the center of the floor again. A shadow fell across her lap, and she looked up to see Roger standing before her.

"Would you care to dance?" he asked.

"I would rather sit this one out. Do you mind?"

"Not at all." He took the empty chair beside her. "I will say, the Americans know how to throw a good party."

She laughed before replying, "Indeed."

"But you looked unhappy when I approached. Is something wrong?"

The smile left her lips as she glanced once more around the barn, looking for the only face she wanted to see.

"Mr. Coltrane?" Roger asked.

She met his gaze. "Yes. I . . . we . . . I—" She felt the sudden urge to cry.

"Not simply a friend then?"

She recalled her conversation with Roger the

previous Sunday and shook her head. "No, I don't want him to be simply a friend. I want ever so much more than that."

"But he doesn't feel the same?"

"Perhaps he might, but he won't admit it even if he does. He believes I deserve someone better than him."

"Perhaps you do. I happen to think you are quite special and deserving of the very best."

She shook her head, frustration welling inside of her again. "There is no one better than him. Not for me."

"Amanda." Roger covered her folded hands with one of his own. "You do not know him well enough to say that."

"But I do. He's rescued me. Twice. I could have died either time, and he risked his own life to save me. We spent days riding together through the wilderness of Yellowstone. I know him better than I know many of the men who wanted to court me back in England. Men my father would have willingly allowed me to marry."

"Men of your class."

"There are no classes in America," she said with a defiant tilt of her chin. "It's one of the things I love most about this country."

"Not entirely true. Perhaps less so in a place like this, but class differences still exist, even in this country."

"It doesn't matter. I don't want any of them. No other man has interested me. Not ever. None of them have made me feel . . . anything."

"Feelings are well and good, my friend, and I hope you find love in your future marriage. But there is more to consider than feelings before you pledge the rest of your life to another." Roger looked toward the dancing couples spinning past them in time with a lively tune. "I wish Sebastian were here."

Amanda did not share his sentiment. While she loved her brother dearly, she knew he would join William and Roger in their objections to Isaiah. He wouldn't think Isaiah was good enough for her either. And so she was thankful Sebastian was far away, across a continent and an ocean.

However, it would be wonderful if she could talk to her sister-in-law. Jocelyn had fallen in love with a man no one—including herself—expected her to marry. It had been quite a different situation from her own, but Jocelyn would have had good advice for her all the same.

"Come on." Roger rose and faced her, hand out. "We've talked enough. Let's join the dance and forget your troubles for a while."

She drew a quick breath, then offered the hint of a smile as she took his hand. He was right. They might as well dance. She would solve nothing, sitting there in the corner of the barn, not even knowing where Isaiah was. Tonight she would try to enjoy the party. In the morning, perhaps she would think of a way to make Isaiah love her and to make others accept this decision of her heart.

Chapter Twenty

Amanda didn't come up with a way to make Isaiah love her by the next morning, but lying in the bed, staring at the ceiling as fingers of light began to inch across it, she was convinced she would succeed. After all, her father had been dead set against her coming to America. Even Sebastian had his doubts about bringing her along on this trip. But here she was. If she could make the dream of visiting the Old West happen, she could win the heart of the man she already loved. She was nothing if not determined.

Roger thought she didn't know Isaiah well enough to be certain he was the only man for her. He was wrong, of course, but perhaps getting to know Isaiah better was part of the answer.

"So I need to spend more time with him," she said aloud. "He needs to know me better as well."

But how could she make that happen? And how much time was left before his ankle was healed? Knowing his determination, he might pack up his belongings and leave the instant he could put his left foot in the stirrup. Did she have enough time to win his heart before that happened?

Lord, send an early winter. Cover the ground in snow. Do whatever You must to keep him here. Please.

Oh, how utterly selfish of her, to pray for bitter weather. How unkind for the men who worked on this ranch, wanting an early winter just so she could keep Isaiah Coltrane in close proximity.

I'm sorry, Lord. I do not wish to be selfish. I only want more time with him.

She pushed aside the blankets and sat up, her legs and feet dangling over the side of the bed. The air was chilly, the warmth of the previous day forgotten overnight, and the cool temperature of the room hurried her through her morning ablutions. Finally, dressed and ready for the day, she went to the window and looked outside. She was on the wrong side of the house to see the sun rise over the mountain range, but sunlight gilded the treetops outside her window and the grasslands farther away had turned from gray to tan as day arrived.

Father, I know what my heart feels. I want Isaiah to love me in return. Am I wrong to ask for Your help?

Seek God and He will answer. That's what the Bible told her. But she wasn't sure that she knew how to hear His voice. Could He have spoken to her already, and she'd missed what He said? Jesus said His sheep knew His voice. She was one of His sheep, but was she as attuned to His voice as she should be? As she needed to be?

DRESSED AND READY FOR CHURCH, Isaiah stood at the window of the cottage's parlor. Although he stared outside, his thoughts lingered on the previous day and Amanda's declaration of her feelings, her voice clear as if she were speaking to him now.

"I want a man who stands on a mountain trail on a foggy Sunday morning and quotes Scripture in praise to God."

He remembered that Sunday morning in Yellowstone during their trek along the Mary Mountain Trail. Not because it had been unusual. He often felt God's presence when he was in the wilderness and responded by quoting words from the Bible. How could he not respond with praise at such moments when surrounded by the beauty of nature? But Amanda's soft amen had imprinted that particular moment on his heart.

Yes, he wanted more than friendship, but it wasn't wise to feel that way.

He gave his head a slow shake, and the present came into focus. The surrey now waited outside the front door of the main house, the team of horses standing patiently, only their tails in motion. He quickly set his hat on his head and reached for the crutches. He'd nearly crossed the barnyard when the front door opened and Amanda stepped into view, looking every bit as lovely as she had the night before, this time wearing a gown of deep emerald green. She hesitated when she saw him. Then, with a lift of her chin and a look of defiance in her dark eyes, she continued down the steps from the porch and toward the surrey.

"Good morning, Amanda." He touched a fingertip to the brim of his hat and found himself wishing they weren't on opposites sides of the buggy.

She stopped again, a look of surprise crossing her face. Was it the use of her given name that caused it? "Good morning, Mr. Coltrane." No, she wasn't over the anger she'd displayed last night. At least not entirely.

"It's a beautiful morning," he added.

She glanced at the sky, as if checking to see if his words were true.

"I imagine there will be plenty of folks at church still talking about last night's barn dance."

She nodded to acknowledge his words but remained silent.

William came out of the house with Mrs. Adler. He said a word of greeting to Isaiah before helping the two women into the surrey, Amanda on the front seat and Mrs. Adler behind her. William rounded the surrey to sit beside Amanda while Isaiah settled next to the housekeeper.

As William took up the reins, he glanced over his shoulder. "Everyone ready?" He didn't wait for an answer before he clicked his tongue and slapped the reins against the horses' rumps. The surrey jerked forward, and they were off toward town.

Isaiah's gaze fastened on Amanda. He had a good view of her profile, and by the set of her shoulders, the lift of her chin, and the firm line of her mouth, he supposed she was aware of it. He broke the silence, saying, "It was nice of Roger to give up his seat in the buggy so I could go to church with you."

William answered, "I believe he was glad for an excuse to sleep in this morning. He enjoyed himself last night."

"I take it he doesn't like to ride horseback."

William thought for a moment, then answered, "I can't recall seeing him in the saddle all this summer."

"Roger *can* ride," Amanda said with a quick glance at William. "But it isn't something he enjoys. Strange really, since Sebastian and Adam love riding so very much. They raced their horses all over the countryside back in England, but Roger never joined them."

"You're like your brothers then," Isaiah said. "You love to ride."

At last this drew her eyes toward him. "Yes." The hint of a smile curved the corner of her mouth. "I do love to ride. Being with horses is one of my favorite things."

He didn't allow himself to smile in return. Not yet. It was too soon. But he was thankful for the sign of a thaw between them. Perhaps he shouldn't be, but he was.

Chapter Twenty-One

I t is against my better judgment to remove the cast on your ankle just yet, Mr. Coltrane." Dr. Grant sat back in his chair in the examination room. "But if I do, you'll need to keep it supported with a splint whenever you are up and about. Weight-bearing needs to be limited. You should keep using your crutches for at least a few more weeks."

"Fine," Isaiah answered. "I'll follow all your directions. But I want the cast off. It's driving me crazy."

The doctor shook his head. "Has anyone told you that you're a troublesome patient, sir?"

Isaiah chuckled.

Dr. Grant rose and retrieved a small saw from a drawer. Isaiah forgot his laughter as the physician instructed him to lay back on the table. "And don't move. I'm going to saw through the plaster of Paris, and I don't want to cut you in the process."

"I don't want that either."

"Once that's done, I'll just break it into pieces. It won't take long to get it removed."

Isaiah lay still, staring at the ceiling, and listened to the sound of the small saw cutting through the hardened gypsum that had encased his ankle for the past three weeks. Three weeks that already felt like a year. It wasn't the cast that drove him crazy, if he was honest. It was the inactivity that came with it. The inability to get up and do whatever he wanted to do when he wanted to do it. Long winters were difficult for the same reason.

Over a week had passed since the barbecue. Over a week since he'd watched Amanda dance in the arms of other men. He'd hated not being able to ask her to dance with him, even when he'd known it was a fool thing to desire.

"Dr. Grant?"

"Hmm?"

"What if I wanted to head back to Montana?"

The doctor stopped. "Do you mean by yourself on horseback?"

"Yes, sir."

"I'd advise against it. That break wasn't as bad as some, but it's not completely healed yet. If you do too much too soon, put too much weight on it, you could cause further injury. You could do yourself harm. It could become an injury that will trouble you the rest of your life. You're a young man. You think you're invincible, but you're not. You don't want to go through life with a constant limp, not to mention that you might have to live with pain."

"It was just a thought. I won't do it until you give me the go-ahead."

And the truth was, he didn't want to leave Eden's Gate. He didn't want to say goodbye to Amanda. Not any sooner than he had to.

OCTOBER HAD BROUGHT NOTICEABLY COOLER temperatures to the valley. For the first time since Amanda arrived at Eden's Gate, she needed to wear a jacket in midday while working with Ebony.

"She's looking good," William called to Amanda as he walked toward the corral.

She reined in, stopping the mare, then reached down to stroke the horse's neck. "I'm pleased with her progress."

"You should be."

She dismounted and led the mare toward the fence where William stood.

"Maybe I could hire you to work with some of the other young horses we've got."

"Hire me?" She laughed. "You wouldn't have to do that."

"Couldn't have you do it for free. Remember, you and Roger are paying guests on this ranch."

"William, I am no longer a paying guest. I'm a member of your family. You and I are related. Our siblings are married. Remember?"

"I remember."

"And I would love to work with your horses. I would love to help any way I can."

His eyes narrowed as he studied her. "You mean that, don't you?"

"Of course I mean it. Why wouldn't I?"

"It isn't . . . what I expected when I first met you."

William didn't have to explain what he meant. Amanda understood. He'd expected her to be a lady of leisure, wanting to be waited on, her every need attended to by others. She was glad she'd surprised him. She could play that part when she had to, but it wasn't who she truly was or who she wanted to be. Not any longer. Perhaps it never had been. Her gaze flicked toward the cottage. Isaiah needed to understand that as well.

"He isn't back from town yet," William said.

"Town?"

"He went to see Dr. Grant."

"Did he go alone?"

"Yeah. Drove the buggy. He's hoping to get the cast off, he said."

"Isn't it too soon for that?"

He shrugged in answer.

She patted Ebony's neck again, pressed her forehead to the same spot, then straightened and looked at William. "I love him," she said softly. "You've warned me against it. Roger's warned me against it. For that matter, Isaiah's warned me against it. None of those warnings matter. I love him anyway."

William shook his head, as if trying to deny her confession.

"Remember when you asked me if I would want him to return to England with me? I didn't answer then, but I can answer now. No, I would not want to do that. I want him to stay in America, and I want to stay with him. I want to live here."

"Amanda." He said her name slowly.

"It's what I want, William."

"Sebastian will never agree to it."

"I do not need his permission. I am a grown woman. I have a little money of my own. I can make my own choices. And if you don't want me to remain on Eden's Gate because of my decision, I will find somewhere else to live." Of course, she hoped there wouldn't be any question of where she would go from here. She hoped she would be with Isaiah, wherever he was.

WITH BANDIT RIDING beside him on the buggy seat, Isaiah clucked to the gelding. The horse didn't need much encouragement to break into a fast trot, not with the house and barn in view, and it wasn't long before they arrived in the barnyard. He saw Amanda in the corral with Ebony.

William, who stood outside the corral, turned at the sound of the arriving vehicle, and he raised a hand before saying something to Amanda. Then he walked toward the buggy. "Is the cast gone?"

"It is. Dr. Grant replaced it with a splint. Gives me a little more freedom. I can unwrap it when I'm in bed, feel the air on my skin." He looked toward the corral and saw Amanda step into the saddle. "Ebony's coming along."

William looked in the same direction. "Yes. That's what I said."

Isaiah motioned for Bandit to get down before he did the same, taking care to keep the weight off his left ankle. Once the crutches were beneath his arms, he turned toward William. "I wondered if there's something I can do around here to pull my own weight, despite these crutches."

"It isn't necessary for you to help out. It was your smart thinking that got us on the trail of the rustlers. You've done more than enough."

"Might not be necessary in your mind, but it is for me."

William frowned. "Let me think on it. I'll let you know." Then he began to free the gelding from its harness.

Isaiah observed the unhitching for only a moment before he found his attention drawn to the corral where Amanda loped Ebony in a circle. Her long, dark hair was braided, and the thick hank bounced against her back, keeping time with the horse's motion. As beautiful as she'd looked the night of the barn dance, she looked even more beautiful on horseback. Images of their days in Yellowstone swept through his mind once again, and he wondered, for an instant, if she could be happy in a different way of life from the one she'd always known.

She reined in, drawing Ebony to an abrupt halt and pulling Isaiah from his own thoughts.

"Your cast is gone," she shouted.

He moved toward the corral. "It is."

"Does it feel better?"

"Yes, but I'm still stuck with a splint and these crutches for a couple more weeks at least. Can't get my foot back in a boot yet either. Too swollen."

"The time will go fast. You'll be much better soon."

Odd, how he hoped for the swift passage of time while also wanting it to stand still. Because when his ankle healed, when the doctor said it was all right for him to do so, he would pack up his belongings, including everything Paddy had brought to the ranch, and return to his cabin in Montana. Alone.

How could it be otherwise?

Chapter Twenty-Two

Three letters arrived from England the following day. As soon as Logan Coe placed them in Amanda's hands, she rushed to her bedroom to read them in private. Seated at the writing desk, she opened each envelope, then arranged the letters in the order they'd been written and mailed.

---

9 September 1895
Dear Amanda,

Jocelyn and I arrived at Hooke Manor two days ago. We had rough seas on the Atlantic which slowed our crossing. Jocelyn is a great sailor and never minded the storms. In truth, I believe she relished them. But you know her nature.

It feels quite strange to be back in England and even more strange to be at Hooke Manor without

Father, knowing he will never be with us again. I have already had a meeting with Bramston, Father's attorney, and have been apprised of all of my legal responsibilities as the earl. Nothing new or surprising to me. Father kept me informed of what would be expected when this day came. I simply did not believe it would come this soon.

It is good to be with Adam and Eliza again. They are both well, and Adam is looking forward to the arrival of Ebony when you return in the spring. We all look forward to that day. I was given permission to share Adam and Eliza's happy news. They are expecting a baby in early spring. Perhaps you will be back in time for the birth. Eliza hopes so. Of course, you could return sooner and be with the family for Christmas. Please think about that.

Give William, Roger, and everyone on Eden's Gate our best wishes.

Your brother,
Sebastian

A BABY. Adam and Eliza were going to have a baby. What wonderful, absolutely delightful news. And in the spring. She was supposed to return to Hooke Manor in the spring. Everyone expected it. Sebastian even hoped she would come sooner. Disappointment awaited him.

She opened the second envelope.

14 September 1895
Dear Amanda,

I received your letter of 21 August and was
dismayed to learn you were leaving on the tour of
Yellowstone National Park as planned, despite all
the advice that you should not go. I realize by the
time you receive this letter, you will have long since
returned from the park. While I do not believe it
was wise for you to go on your own, I do hope the
excursion was everything you wanted it to be. I
hope it helped to ease your grief over Father's
death.

Jocelyn has settled into her role as the Countess
of Hooke and is already a favorite of everyone who
has met her, from servants to the titled gentry.
Many friends and acquaintances have paid calls
since learning of our return. They come to share
condolences over Father's death but also because
they want to see my American wife for themselves.
Some, I venture to say, come expecting to dismiss
her out of hand, but she charms them, one and all.
You would be proud of her. I must add that Jocelyn
and Eliza have already become good friends.

I confess that Hooke Manor does not feel quite
like home without you here. Please consider ending
your stay in America and come home sooner than
the spring. You are asked after by many, including
several young gentlemen. Courtship would have to

wait until the end of our period of mourning, of course, but they are eager to see you again.

Before I close, I must tell you that I am happier than I ever expected to be, thanks to my marriage to Jocelyn. I would like to see you experience the same kind of happiness. I hope seeing our joy will make you want it too.

Again, please consider an early return. We would love to have you with us for Christmas.

Your brother,
Sebastian

LONGING FLARED IN HER HEART. She missed Sebastian and Jocelyn. She missed Adam and Eliza. She missed Hooke Manor and the horses and the woods and the tenant farmers and the nearby village and its residents. But she didn't want to go home early. She didn't want to go home at all. Not if it meant leaving Isaiah. Not as long as she had a shred of hope of making him learn to love her too.

She opened the last envelope.

23 September 1895
Dearest Amanda,

We received your letter of 5 September, and I

was somewhat alarmed by what you wrote but even more by what you did not tell us. Please share more of the details of your adventure in the park. You had to be rescued from the river? You must explain. I cannot wait until you are able to tell me in person. At the moment, I question the wisdom of allowing you to remain in America at all. You should be with us and soon.

I am sorry to learn the cattle thieves returned to the area. I pray they have been tracked down at last. Having helped Jocelyn with the ranch's record-keeping, I have a good understanding what those losses mean to Eden's Gate and the other ranchers.

Jocelyn and I leave tomorrow for London. We won't attend Lord and Lady Blakeslee's Autumn Ball or other social events, of course, since we are still in full mourning. But it will give me an oppor-tunity to introduce my wife to a few more people whom I would like her to know.

I look forward to your next letter.

Your brother,
Sebastian

GUILT TWISTED IN HER BELLY. How could she have put on her favorite gown and danced on the day of the barbecue? How could she have forgotten all the rules of mourning that had been ingrained in her from girlhood? Her father had passed away less than two months ago, but she hadn't avoided the big social event as she should have. Most days she wore simple attire—a plain blouse, a brown skirt, and boots for riding—but she wasn't clad all in black. Did that mean she'd loved her father any less? No, it didn't. But Sebastian would be ashamed of her, all the same.

Tears blurring her vision, she placed the three letters on the desk, then folded her hands on her lap and bowed her head. She didn't pray, only sat in silence. Waiting, perhaps, for answers to questions she didn't have the heart to ask.

———

THE BARNYARD WAS DESERTED that afternoon as Isaiah led Buck to the hitching post. He managed to brush the gelding, then get the blanket and saddle onto him, without putting any weight on his bad ankle throughout the process. That pleased him. Would please the doctor too, he imagined.

"Need help?"

His heart reacted to the sound of Amanda's voice as usual, but he forced himself not to look over his shoulder. "No thanks. I've got it."

"I daresay you do. I suppose this means you intend to go for a ride."

"It does."

"How extraordinary!"

"Extraordinary?"

"You're wearing your boot."

He looked down at his foot. "Not my boot.

Borrowed from someone. Chuck, I think. William brought it to me yesterday."

"Whosoever boot it is, it is allowing you to be on your horse. That's good. May I join you? The day is rather fine. Too fine to be indoors."

He'd planned to ride alone. He'd hoped some time in the saddle and the sun and wind on his face would blow this very woman from his thoughts where she'd been lodged for too long.

Before he could refuse her request, she said, "I shall get Ebony ready."

There was no point arguing. She would do as she pleased. And, in truth, he didn't want to argue. He would have to blow her from his thoughts another time.

When both horses were saddled and bridled, Isaiah realized he had something else to trouble him. How to mount Buck without putting too much weight on his bad ankle. He couldn't put his left foot in the stirrup and step up that way. That would put weight where it shouldn't be. He couldn't mount from the right because that would leave his left foot on the ground while putting his right in the stirrup, again putting weight where he shouldn't.

Seeing his dilemma, Amanda said, "There's a mounting block in the barn. Shall I get it for you?"

Irritated by the suggestion, he grasped the saddle horn with both hands and swung into the saddle, using the strength of his arms more than his legs. Although the arms weren't enough, given the pain that shot up his leg. Dr. Grant would no longer be pleased with him.

"Where are we going?" Amanda asked as she turned Ebony around.

He pointed. "The ridge. That oughta be far enough for my first day back in the saddle."

They nudged the horses and rode away from the barn.

The cool nights of recent weeks had transformed the landscape, splattering shades of red, yellow, and gold among the green, and the sight of it stirred his soul. "'When I consider thy heavens, the work of thy fingers, the moon and the stars, which thou hast ordained; What is man, that thou art mindful of him? And the son of man, that thou visitest him?'"

"I love it when you do that."

He glanced her way. "Do what?"

"Quote the Scriptures. Like it is a conversation between you and the Lord. I find it quite beautiful."

Her simple words tugged at his heart again. Something she did so easily. But that didn't change reality. It didn't change how impossible a future would be for the two of them. No matter how much it might be what he wanted. Heartbreak was inevitable. Bad enough for him. He didn't want her to feel it too. If he could only make her see that. Looking out for her had become a habit, and he wanted to protect her in this as well as from rivers and cliffs. If he just knew the right words to say to her—

Amanda, as if wanting to distract him before he could find those words, said, "William told me he and the boys will begin the cattle drive on Monday."

"They ship them to market out of Pocatello, right?"

"Yes."

"Jake says they're moving the herd to the south range this week. Wish I could have helped." He gave his head a small shake, realizing she had succeeded in distracting him with only a single comment, making him talk about driving cattle and riding with the cowboys instead of telling her the two of them could never be more than friends, that their lives must diverge and must do so soon.

WITH THEIR HORSES stopped at the top of the ridge, the rangeland spilling out below them until it swept up into the foothills, Amanda stared at Isaiah while he stared at the beautiful landscape.

Oh, my love. I know you want to dissuade me. But it shall not work. My heart is yours, even if you leave me. It shall never belong to another.

A lump formed in her throat, and she found herself dangerously close to tears. Somehow she must make him see, make him understand. Not only that she loved him, but that he loved her too. And wasn't it strange that she could see what he felt even before he saw it himself?

She looked away from him and took a deep breath.

That had to be it. His efforts to push her away had to be because he didn't recognize the depth of his own feelings. Once he saw for himself that he loved her, that they were meant to be together, he would declare his feelings and their future would be secured.

I will be patient. I will pray. I will make him see. I will. God in heaven, help me make him see.

Chapter Twenty-Three

21 October 1895

Dearest Sebastian and Jocelyn,

I wish you, Sebastian, could see for yourself the glorious colors of autumn in Idaho. Perhaps Jocelyn can describe how this valley and the mountains look at this time of year. The changing foliage kept Roger at his easel for days at a time as he tried to capture all of the golds, reds, and oranges that filled the mountainsides. Some of his paintings are incredible, as you will see for yourself when he returns. Perhaps he will need to have a private ship in order to get them all back to England.

However, the beautiful colors are nearly gone now, the leaves falling to the earth, and Roger has journeyed to the capital city for a few weeks. He met a fellow artist while in Yellowstone during the summer, and he was invited to stay with the man in Boise City for a month. I will be eager to see the paintings he does during his visit to the western side of this state.

With William and many of the cowboys also gone, driving the cattle to market, the ranch has been far too quiet. Mr. Kincaid seems out of sorts because he has so few people to cook for. I would think he would be glad for less work, but that does not seem to be the case.

I have begun working with some of the younger horses on the ranch. I believe Adam would be proud of me, although I will never be as skilled a trainer as he is. I ride Ebony every day, and she has progressed wonderfully in the months since you left Eden's Gate.

At breakfast this morning, Mrs. Adler told me she expects snow to fall today. It does feel cold enough for it. Although she seems to dread it, I am looking forward to seeing the land blanketed in white. My first winter in America. It already feels quite magical to me. Oh, how I love it. While I miss you both, along with Adam and Eliza, I feel at home here. I do not miss the balls and soirees or paying obligatory calls on members of society. I do not miss the bustle of London during the season. I have fallen very much in love with Idaho and the Tetons and Yellowstone.

Your loving sister,

Amanda

The first snowfall of the season came to Eden's Gate on the day Dr. Grant told Isaiah he no longer had to wear a splint to support his ankle. When the two men walked out of the cottage, lazy snowflakes drifted to earth, light and airy, but both men knew the storm could worsen in a heartbeat.

"I'd best get on my way back to town," the doctor said. "Remember to take it easy on that ankle. Just because the splint's off doesn't mean you should behave as if it was never broken. There's still healing to be done. You can be done with the crutches, but use the cane as much as you can."

"I'll be careful."

"Is William back from the cattle drive yet?" They reached the buggy, and Dr. Grant set his bag on the floor of the vehicle before stepping up to the seat.

"Not yet," Isaiah answered, "but if all went well, he and the boys should be back later today or tomorrow."

"That's good." The doctor looked up at the gray clouds. "They don't want to be out there in this weather if they can keep from it."

Isaiah took a step back from the buggy, nodding in agreement. He didn't want to be riding in bad weather either, but that might be what he had to do. He was free of the splint, and he could ride. True, he still wore a borrowed boot because of the swelling, but the doctor said it would decrease a little more each day. Was a swollen foot enough to keep him on Eden's Gate a few more days? Another week perhaps?

Dr. Grant clucked to the horse as he gently slapped the reins against its rump. The buggy moved forward.

Within moments it disappeared around the corner of the barn.

"Is the splint gone?"

Isaiah turned toward the front porch. Amanda stood at the railing, a dark shawl wrapped around her shoulders. Like a moth to a flame, he moved toward her. "It's gone." He glanced down at his mismatched boots that were now dusted with snow. "But I'm going to owe Chuck a new pair of boots."

"Do you suppose this snowstorm will last?" Amanda asked. "Will it keep William and the others from getting home?"

"Shouldn't last. Not this early in the year. But you never know."

"Why don't you come inside, out of the cold?"

Before he could answer, he heard a sound that caused him to turn. His gaze swept the barnyard, not sure at first what he looked for. Then he heard it again. A whimper. More than a whimper. The sound of an animal in pain.

The curtain of falling snow had grown thicker, but finally he saw movement on the west side of the barn. He felt a hitch in his chest. Bandit? He moved as quickly as the cane allowed in that direction. Amanda caught up with him before he reached the dog, and he heard her quick intake of breath even as he felt his own pulse jump. It was Bandit, and the white on his faithful friend's chest was stained with blood.

"Hey, fella." Isaiah dropped the cane as he reached for the dog.

"Don't," Amanda said, her voice stern. "You

shouldn't carry him. It's too much weight on your bad ankle. I'll get him." She gathered the injured dog into her arms.

"Take him to the cottage." Leaving the cane behind, he limped toward the guest quarters.

Inside, Amanda laid the dog on the table in the corner of the parlor.

"You're covered in his blood. Your clothes will be ruined."

She glanced down. "That doesn't matter. It's more important that we stop his bleeding." Her fingers freed the buttons of her stained blouse.

"What are you doing?"

"It's ruined anyway. We can use it to bind that wound." She pulled the blouse loose from the waistband of her skirt, then shrugged out of it.

At fancy dress balls in the east, Isaiah had seen fully clothed women who'd revealed more skin and feminine attributes than Amanda did now. The chemise she'd worn beneath the blouse had a high neck and short sleeves. Nonetheless, the sight of her in the undergarment—faintly stained with blood—stirred something inside of him, made him forget Bandit's injuries, if only for a moment.

"Isaiah, get some water to cleanse the wounds." She pressed the blouse against the worst of Bandit's wounds, trying to staunch the bleeding.

He should have told her to leave the cottage. He should have told her he would take care of his dog. Instead, he went to his bedroom and retrieved the water jar and a towel. When he returned, he placed the jar on the table before reaching for a lamp, bringing it closer for a better view.

Still pressing the ruined blouse against the wound, Amanda put her face close to the dog's ear. "You'll be all right, boy. Lie still now. We will take care of you, I promise." When she straightened, she held out a hand. "Please give me the lamp. I shall hold it while you do whatever you must. I've never sewn anything that was living. I do not believe I can."

Again, Isaiah did as she asked. Bandit whimpered as his wounds were bathed but didn't move otherwise.

"What happened to him?" she asked softly, holding the lamp as close as possible while keeping it out of the way.

"I'm guessing he tangled with a wolf. A bear would have done more damage than this." He wiped another spot. "These wounds are from teeth, not claws."

"Poor boy," she crooned as she caressed the dog's head again.

Once the blood was washed away and the worst of the wounds stitched closed, Isaiah felt some of the tension drain from him. The injuries weren't as serious as they could have been. The dog's right ear was torn, a piece of it missing, but there was nothing he could do for that. No bones appeared to be broken. Still, it must have taken great effort and determination for Bandit to return to the ranch house in such a condition.

As if to confirm his master's thoughts, the dog lifted his head, whimpered again, then let his head drop back onto the table.

Amanda set down the lamp. "Will he be all right?"

"Yes. He'll probably be weak from blood loss for a while, but he'll recover."

She reached to touch Isaiah's arm. "And are you all right?"

"It's usually me who gets hurt." He released a humorless chuckle. "Bandit's the smart one of the two of us."

Sympathy laced her smile. "We'll take good care of him. You two can heal together."

It was only then he realized how close to him she stood. Close enough that he couldn't look away. Close enough to offer the comfort he longed for. His arms—somehow around her by this time—drew her even closer.

THE TOUCH of Isaiah's lips sent heat coursing through Amanda's body. For weeks, she'd wondered what it might be like to be kissed by him. She'd wanted it to happen, hoped for it to happen. But this . . . this was unlike anything she'd imagined. The strength drained from her body, and if not for his arms holding her so close against him, she would have crumpled to the floor.

Was it like this for every man and woman the first time they kissed? She'd never been kissed before. Not by a man on the mouth. Her father and brother, even Roger and William, had kissed her cheek on occasion. This was not the same at all. How could she have known it would be so different? How could she have *not* known?

A soft groan in Isaiah's throat made her want to do

the same. Perhaps she did do the same. Drawing his head back, he whispered her name.

A shiver ran up her spine, and she rose on tiptoes to press her lips against his once more, wrapping her arms around his neck, unable to bear the slightest separation, not even for a moment. With another groan, his arms pulled her close again. Oh, the strength of him. Oh, the warmth of him. Oh, the—

"What on earth is going on here!"

In unison, their heads turned toward the doorway of the cottage.

Mrs. Adler stepped into the parlor, her expression sparking with umbrage. "Have you lost all sense of propriety, Mr. Coltrane?"

Isaiah released his hold on Amanda and took a step back. Cold air whirled around her. Was it from the absence of his embrace or from the open door? She didn't care the reason. She simply wanted to be back in his arms.

The housekeeper gasped, her indignation changing to a look of horror. "What has he done to you, Miss Amanda? Are you bleeding? Your clothes—"

She followed the older woman's gaze to her chemise. Pink stains marred the white fabric. "He's done nothing, Mrs. Adler. It's from the dog. Bandit's been hurt. Not I." As she spoke, she stepped back, revealing the table and the dog lying on it, her bloodied blouse lying in a heap beside Bandit. "I was … helping Mr. Coltrane."

"It wasn't helping a dog that I witnessed." The housekeeper pointed a finger at Isaiah. "You are not to be trusted, sir. I should've known it. You aren't used to living in polite society, and now you've taken liberties with an innocent girl. But you'll not get away with it. Mr. William will hear of this when he returns, and you'll get your comeuppance." She grabbed the shawl from the floor—when had it fallen there?—and wrapped it around Amanda's shoulders.

Amanda allowed herself to be pulled out of the cottage, across the barnyard, and into the main house. But once in the parlor, she broke free of the housekeeper's grasp. "Mrs. Adler, leave me be. You don't understand."

"I understand plenty, miss. More than you think. I also understand that your brother would want me to look after you. Especially in Mr. William's absence."

"I am not a child."

"No, you aren't. And that makes what I saw in the cottage all the more alarming."

"It was only a kiss," she said softly. But even as the words passed her lips, they felt like a lie.

"He disrobed you."

"He did not. I removed my blouse. I used it to staunch the blood."

Mrs. Adler didn't seem to hear the explanation. "What happened in Yellowstone Park? You were alone with him on the trail. Did he take advantage of you?"

"No. Of course not. Nothing happened."

"I should've known right then. Everyone was so thankful that a professional guide brought you safely home again. But we should've known he wasn't to be trusted."

"Isaiah has never been anything but a gentleman

with me." She whirled away and darted up the stairs. Once in her room, the door closed behind her, she threw herself onto the bed and burst into tears, unsure why she cried yet unable to keep from it.

Later, tears spent, she rolled onto her back, staring up at the ceiling. Was it truly so terrible? Yes, she had removed her blouse, but she hadn't been naked. She'd removed it to help an injured animal. Any woman might have done the same in a crisis. Yes, Isaiah had kissed her, but she'd kissed him back. She loved him. How could it be so wrong for them to share a kiss? Mrs. Adler had appeared scandalized by what she'd seen, but no liberties had been taken. Amanda had always felt safe in Isaiah's company. From the moment he'd snatched her from the river, she'd felt safe. He would never have forced himself upon her, never have harmed her in any way. They hadn't done anything wrong, in Yellowstone or in the cottage.

Heat rose in her cheeks. She might be unmarried, but she wasn't entirely ignorant of what happened between a man and a woman. Or what *could* happen between them. But nothing *had* happened. Nothing but a few kisses.

Oh, those kisses. She hadn't known all that a kiss could do. She hadn't dreamed she would feel the touch of his lips all the way to her toes, that her stomach would whirl, that her legs would go weak.

And all she wanted right now was for him to kiss her again.

Chapter Twenty-Four

The next morning, Isaiah knocked on the front door of the main house. A short while later, it opened, revealing a stern Mrs. Adler.

He removed his hat. "I would like to talk with Miss Whitcombe."

"I don't think that's a good idea." She crossed her arms over her chest.

"All the same, I would like to speak with her."

She huffed her disapproval before taking a step back and opening the door wider. Astonished by her acquiescence—he'd believed it possible that she would slam the door in his face—he entered the house and stood in the middle of the parlor. The housekeeper shot him a sharp glance before climbing the stairs.

Isaiah had lain awake throughout the night, considering again and again what Mrs. Adler had witnessed and what she'd said to them. He had to confess, to himself and to God, that his own desires might have carried them too far if they hadn't been interrupted.

The truth was, he'd lusted after Amanda in his heart even if not by his actions. He'd carelessly risked her reputation. It didn't matter that the barnyard had been empty of cowboys, that it was unlikely they'd been seen going into the cottage together. It didn't matter that their concern, at least at first, had been for the injured dog. The moment she'd removed her blood-stained blouse and he'd failed to stop her, he had put her at risk. Taking her in his arms and kissing her had only worsened the situation and made her more vulnerable to gossip and ruination.

"Isaiah?"

He lifted his gaze to the top of the stairs. Amanda stood there, wearing a dark blue gown, her expression a mixture of hope, fear, and confusion.

"Thank you for seeing me." He ran the fingers of one hand through his hair as he watched her descend.

"How is Bandit?" She stopped at the bottom of the stairs and folded her hands at her waist.

He was aware of Mrs. Adler, watching from above, but he didn't move his gaze from Amanda. "He's all right. Limping a little. Like me."

Her smile was there and gone.

"I came to apologize, Amanda. For what happened yesterday."

"Apologize?" she whispered.

"Yes. And to say I want to make things right."

"Make things right?" she echoed again.

He lowered his voice, wanting his words to be only for her. "I've come to ask you to marry me."

Her eyes widened, and she sucked in a soft breath.

"I don't have a lot to offer. I've told you that before. But what I do have would be yours. Above all, my name would be yours. No one would be able to speak against you or accuse you of any sort of impropriety." Now he glanced up in the direction of the housekeeper. From her expression, he hadn't changed her opinion of him, whether or not she'd heard his proposal. He returned his gaze to Amanda. "We can be married as soon as you wish."

"Yes, Isaiah. I will marry you." She took a step toward him. "And I wish to marry you today."

His heart hammered in his chest, surprised by the swiftness of her response. Although he shouldn't be. She'd made her feelings clear on the night of the barbecue. Still, as he'd told her then, as he'd told her in the weeks since, and as he'd told her moments ago, he had little to offer a lady. He was a simple man. He led a simple life. But he could offer her protection. He could offer fidelity. He could treasure her as she deserved.

"I will get my wrap. We can go now." She turned and also looked up. "Please come with us, Mrs. Adler, to be my witness."

"Witness?" the woman responded.

"To our marriage."

"Marriage? Miss Amanda, don't be rash. Surely that isn't the solution."

"You said yourself that you didn't want Mr. Coltrane to get away with—what was it?—taking liberties."

The change in Amanda's tone surprised Isaiah even

more than her quick agreement to marry him. She sounded . . . happy? eager? excited?

More doubts sprang to life. Offering to marry her after they'd been discovered in a passionate embrace, Amanda half-clothed, was the right thing to do. Or was it? She fancied herself in love with him. But was what she felt love? Love enough for the life she would be forced to live as his wife. And after they wed, where would they go? How long would they remain on Eden's Gate? Would he pack her up and take her to his Montana cabin right away? There was little in the way of food there, considering how long he'd been away. He would need to hunt game to feed them through the winter. Would he leave her alone for days at a time while he hunted? She wasn't ready to fend for herself in a cabin in the wilderness. Especially with months of winter ahead of them. The two of them, alone in that rustic cabin.

"Isaiah."

He blinked and focused on the beautiful young woman before him.

"I *want* to marry you. I will get my wrap." With that she turned and hurried up the stairs.

HEART POUNDING, Amanda reached her room, closing the door firmly behind her lest Mrs. Adler decide to follow. She'd seen the doubts enter Isaiah's eyes in those last few moments. She'd seen him wrestling with whether or not marrying her was the best idea. She didn't want him to change his mind. She couldn't allow him to withdraw his proposal.

But he's only marrying you because he thinks he should. He hasn't said he loves you.

She turned and pressed her forehead against the door, an ache tightening like a band around her heart. "I love him, but I've never told him so," she whispered. "It could be the same for him."

But was it? Did he love her?

She remembered the way he'd held her close against him. She remembered the feel of his lips upon hers and the hunger for more that had welled inside.

If he doesn't love me now, I will make him love me in time.

She straightened and walked toward the wardrobe, pausing for a moment to check her appearance in the mirror. Her hair was neat. Her dress was appropriate for the occasion. Nothing like what she would have worn if she'd wed a titled gentleman in a grand ceremony in England, of course, but that had never been what she'd wanted. Especially not after meeting Isaiah.

Drawing in a deep breath, she grabbed her wrap and left the room. Her heart nearly stopped beating when she didn't see Isaiah waiting for her in the parlor.

"He went to prepare the carriage for us," Mrs. Adler said.

"Oh." She sucked in a relieved breath. "I see."

"I think we should wait for Mr. William's return before you do this."

"No, we won't wait for William." She started down the stairs. "We can't be sure when he will be back. It could be today or tomorrow. It might even be longer."

"Miss Amanda—"

"I love Isaiah, Mrs. Adler, and I intend to marry him. Today."

The housekeeper huffed her disapproval. "You are even more headstrong than Miss Joss. She was stubborn too, but you are worse. I'll come and be your witness, but only because I know you will do it without me if I refuse."

Amanda laughed softly, although her heart wasn't in it. "Yes, I believe I am more stubborn than Jocelyn. And yes, I would find another witness if you refuse to come with me." She led the way to the front door.

Gray clouds shrouded the mountains in the east and hung low over the valley. The snow that had fallen yesterday was gone, but there was a promise of more in the air. She saw Isaiah leading the horse and covered surrey toward the front porch. His expression was nearly as grim as Mrs. Adler's. But Amanda meant to change that. He thought he had little to offer her, but all she wanted was to be with him. She didn't care where they lived or how they lived. He thought she would change her mind, that she would find life too hard. She understood without him telling her so. But he was wrong. He was so very, very wrong.

Isaiah offered a hand to help her into the surrey. Then he did the same with Mrs. Adler who harrumphed at him before reluctantly accepting the hand up. Both women covered their skirts with lap robes, and before long, they were on their way.

As the horse trotted toward Gibeon, Amanda's thoughts went to her brother's wedding day. Nearly three months before, Sebastian and Jocelyn had married in the Eden's Gate parlor. Friends and neighbors had been present. Even her father had been there. The house had been full of joy, everyone smiling and ready to celebrate the newlyweds. She glanced toward Isaiah. He didn't look ready to celebrate anything. He looked more like a man condemned to the gallows.

Have I made a terrible mistake? Should I tell him to turn around and take us home?

But no, she couldn't change her mind. Not because of Mrs. Adler's suspicions and objections. Not because she feared for her own reputation. No, she couldn't refuse because she feared, if she did, she would lose Isaiah forever. His ankle was healing. Soon, he would saddle his buckskin and ride away from the Overstreet ranch, Bandit running ahead of him. He would ride away, and she would never see him again. This was her only chance to keep him with her.

Less than an hour later, Isaiah drew the surrey to a halt before the steps of Gibeon Chapel. In the continuing silence, he helped the two women to the ground, then motioned for them to precede him into the church. They found the reverend replacing a floor board in the narthex.

"Good morning, Reverend Blankenship," Amanda said.

He set aside the hammer and stood. "Well, good morning. What brings you to the church so early on a Tuesday morning?"

Isaiah answered, "Miss Whitcombe and I would like to be married."

The reverend grinned. "Well, that is joyous news. Were you thinking of having the wedding here in church? I'll have to check my calendar, but I'm sure we can find a date that works for you."

"Yes, we would like to marry in the church." Isaiah removed his hat. "Today."

The smile slipped from the reverend's face. "Today?"

"Now, if you are able."

Reverend Blankenship's gaze moved from Isaiah to Amanda to Mrs. Adler.

Amanda saw many questions in his eyes, although he didn't ask them aloud. "Mrs. Adler is here to be my witness," she said quickly.

"I can take care of the license, but two witnesses are required." The reverend looked toward Isaiah expectantly.

"I'm afraid I don't know many people here in town. Guess we should've asked Mr. Kincaid to join us this morning."

Amanda's pulse raced. Would this be what stopped them? Something as simple as one witness too few.

"Not to worry." Reverend Blankenship nodded. "Ed Ford's doing some work for me in the back. I'll go get him."

"Thank you, reverend," Isaiah said. "We appreciate it."

Before walking away, Reverend Blankenship looked once more at Amanda, as if to ask her if she was certain.

I am certain. I am. Hurry. Get Mr. Ford. I am certain.

Chapter Twenty-Five

W*hat have I done?* The question swirled in Amanda's head and heart as the horse pulled the surrey toward the ranch. *What have I done?*

She was Mrs. Isaiah Coltrane. She had what she'd wanted most. She'd become Isaiah's wife. So why wasn't she happy? She loved him. He was a good and caring man.

But he only married me because he felt he had to.

A knot formed in her stomach, and she feared she might be sick. She pressed the fingers of her right hand to her mouth and stared up at the pewter sky, fighting for control.

I love him, God. Why do I feel so wretched?

She glanced to her left to look at Isaiah. To look at her husband. His expression remained as solemn now as it had been all morning. She wished she knew what he was thinking.

Please, Father, help him learn to love me. Please.

A short while later, the surrey rounded the barn at

Eden's Gate. Saddled horses were tied to the corral railing, and several men stood talking outside the bunkhouse.

"Mr. William is back," Mrs. Adler said, stating the obvious.

Isaiah drew the buggy to a stop near the front porch, then glanced at Amanda. "We need to speak to him."

"Yes." The word came out a mere whisper.

He got down from the surrey and rounded the back of the vehicle to help the two women disembark. Then he took hold of Amanda's hand and placed it in the crook of his arm. The sickness she'd felt earlier began to ease.

As they turned toward the house, the front door opened and William came out on the porch. "I wondered where you all had gotten to." He grinned at them as he stepped to the railing. "And from the look of that sky, we all got back in the nick of time."

Mrs. Adler gave William a nod. "Not soon enough." With a curt nod, she went inside.

William's smile faded. "Is something wrong?" His gaze flicked between the pair.

Isaiah answered, "Not wrong, exactly." He moved forward, drawing Amanda with him. They stopped at the porch steps. "But we have something to tell you."

Now the other man frowned.

"Amanda and I were married this morning."

William looked as if he'd been turned to stone.

"We are just back from the church in Gibeon," Isaiah added.

"The reverend performed the ceremony?"

"Yes."

"I see." He turned. "Better come inside, the both of you."

The knot in her stomach became like a boulder, and her grip on Isaiah's arm tightened.

"It's all right," he said softly.

She wanted to believe him. Could she?

They went up the steps and entered the house. William waited for them in the parlor. Mrs. Adler was nowhere to be seen.

After they were all seated, William cleared his throat. "I don't think it is necessary for me to express my surprise. When I left with the cattle, you were hardly speaking to each other, as far as I could tell."

She nodded. "I was angry with him after the barbecue."

"So how did you go from hardly speaking to married in a couple of weeks?"

She looked at Isaiah, uncertain how to answer. Should she tell William everything that had happened? Would Mrs. Adler say what she'd seen in the cottage, casting aspersions on the newlyweds?

"William." Isaiah rested his forearms on his thighs, his hands clasped between his knees. "I promise you, whatever brought about this change in our circumstances, whatever the reason for our marriage, I will always take great care of my wife. I will not let her come to harm or let her do without what's important. She won't have wealth but she'll have all she needs for as long as I draw breath. I swear it to you." He met Amanda's gaze. "I swear it to both of you."

Unshed tears made his image blur before her. Perhaps he didn't love her yet, but she had his promise that he would take great care of her. Surely that was enough.

"Sebastian will blame me for this," William said.

"Sebastian wants my happiness, and I am happy." Tears slid down her cheeks as she spoke.

William looked at her for a long time before asking, "What are your plans now?"

Amanda's pulse quickened. Plans? When Isaiah proposed that morning, she'd thought of nothing except getting married, of going to the church in Gibeon and standing before the reverend and promising to love, honor, and cherish him for the remainder of her life. She hadn't thought about this afternoon or this evening or tomorrow.

Isaiah answered, "I hoped you might have use of another hand here on the ranch. At least for the winter."

She felt a rush of relief, even as she wondered if that was truly what he wanted to do. And if not, would he blame her before this winter was over?

Isaiah didn't look away as he waited for an answer. He didn't know what he would do if William said he wasn't hiring. He had few options and only a little money to his name. As for his cabin in Montana, it wasn't fit for a wife in its present state. Not with winter coming on.

"I suppose I could put you to work," William

answered at last. "Now that your ankle's healed." His gaze flicked to Amanda. "The two of you can live in the guest cottage."

Isaiah didn't glance at his bride, but he felt her stiffen and he suspected she blushed. She probably hadn't given thought to their living arrangements.

Father, she is innocent in many ways, as William warned me once. She could be hurt so easily. Don't let me be the cause of it.

"All right then." William rose from the chair. "Take a few days with your bride. Be ready to start work on Monday."

Isaiah stood and offered his hand. "Thank you."

Somewhat reluctantly, Isaiah thought, William shook it. Then he left the parlor.

Isaiah turned toward Amanda. "Why don't you have a look around the cottage and decide what we might need to make it feel like your home? Then I can help move your things."

"I've seen the cottage." Even if she hadn't blushed before, she was blushing now.

"Yes, but you weren't planning to live there." He reached to take her hand and drew her up from the sofa. "You'll see things differently now."

Once again he offered the crook of his arm, and together they left the house. Although he kept himself from looking in the direction of the bunkhouse, he was aware of the small group of silent men watching them. He guessed they'd been told about the wedding ceremony that had taken place earlier that morning. Did they assume he'd done the next best thing to marrying the boss's sister? Sebastian Whitcombe *had* married the boss's sister and no one held it against him. But he was a British lord with a great deal to offer a woman. Isaiah was a game scout, living more by his wits than anything else.

Maybe I did *take advantage of her.* The thought made his stomach turn to lead.

He'd told himself, as he'd lain awake in bed last night, that he would ask her to marry him in order to protect her reputation. But had his decision been that noble? Or had he proposed because he'd wanted to keep her with him, even knowing he wasn't good enough for her? God forgive him, he suddenly feared it was the latter.

He opened the cottage door, then stepped back to allow her to enter first. She cast him an uncertain smile before doing so. He followed after her, closing the door against the October chill.

Bandit rose from the floor to greet them.

"Hello, boy." She leaned down to stroke the dog's head. "How are you?"

He whimpered and gazed up at her with doleful eyes.

"Better," Isaiah said. "Doesn't seem to be in as much pain as he was yesterday."

Bandit's tail smacked the floor a few times.

"I believe he's playing for sympathy."

"Maybe. But that's okay." Her gaze met Isaiah's. "We're good friends."

She meant she was Bandit's friend. Isaiah knew that. But he had the strangest urge to ask if she would say the same about him, now that he was her husband. Would they remain good friends, despite the hardships she would know? Despite never again living in a grand mansion or having a London season. He'd stolen the future she should have had. How long would it be before she realized it?

He cleared his throat. "Have a look around."

She nodded, and he recognized uncertainty in her eyes before she turned and moved through the quarters.

The parlor was large enough for a table with two ladder-back chairs, a sofa and matching stuffed chair, an end table that held an oil lamp, a narrow bookcase filled with books, and a wood stove. A blue and green rug covered the floor. The bedroom had enough room for a tall wardrobe, another stuffed chair, the bed, and a desk and chair that were situated beneath the window. There was also a water closet, something Isaiah had appreciated when he'd had limited mobility and which seemed all the more important now that Amanda was to live here.

"This will do nicely." She turned to face him. "I suppose we shall take our meals in the main house with William."

He felt a twinge of uncertainty. He hadn't considered that particular aspect of their living arrangement. But Amanda couldn't eat in the bunkhouse, and they couldn't ask Chuck or Mrs. Adler to bring food to them in the cottage several times a day. Eating in the main house was the logical choice. It would also be an uncomfortable one. At least that would be true for Isaiah, knowing William's uncertainty over his union with Amanda. "Yes, I suppose so," he answered at last.

She faced the window. "Oh, look. It's snowing again." She leaned toward the glass. "It looks to be serious this time."

"I believe you're right. The snow could stay around awhile."

She turned to him again. "Should we wait out the storm here?" There was a slight quaver in her voice, and it cut its way into his heart.

"Amanda?"

Yes, she mouthed.

She was the bravest woman he'd ever known, but at the moment, she looked scared. As if this was worse than when she'd found herself clinging to a ledge on the side of a cliff. He'd known how to rescue her then. But instead of her rescuer, now he feared he was the reason she found herself in danger.

God, help me make this right.

Chapter Twenty-Six

T he snowstorm abated late that afternoon, and Amanda was able to move her belongings from the bedroom where she'd stayed since May to the guest cottage where she would stay for at least the winter. Isaiah helped, but she almost wished he hadn't. Having him carry an armload of her clothing felt strange and perhaps a little too intimate for her comfort. Which made her realize there were more intimate moments still to come. Butterflies swarmed in her stomach at the thought.

With the last of her belongings moved, she placed her Bible on the small table next to the bed. Then, drawing a deep breath, she faced her husband. "That's the last of it."

He stood in the connecting doorway between parlor and bedroom, watching her in silence.

The swirling butterflies became even more riotous. "Perhaps we should return to the main house. It won't be long until dinner."

"Good idea. We don't want Mrs. Adler more upset with us than she is already." Was there a note of humor in his voice?

Some of her tension eased, and she offered a smile. "No. We don't want that."

He took a step back, allowing her room to pass through the doorway, and together they left the cottage, walking through the blanket of snow that now covered the barnyard. On the porch, they stomped their feet before entering the house.

"Something smells good," he said as they moved toward the dining room.

She breathed in the delicious aromas wafting from the kitchen, and her stomach responded with a soft growl. But when she entered the dining room, she forgot about hunger. Two places at the table were set with china and crystal. A silver candelabra sat in the center of a pristine white tablecloth, providing illumination.

She exchanged a glance with Isaiah. "Is this for us?"

"Appears so." A smile tipped the corners of his mouth. "Perhaps they aren't as upset with us as we feared."

"Perhaps." Her pulse quickened and her stomach tumbled.

He offered the crook of his arm. "Shall we?"

She didn't want to be escorted to her place at the table. Instead, she wanted him to wrap both arms around her. She wanted him to hold her close and kiss her, the same way he'd kissed her last night. But it didn't happen.

Not long after Isaiah had settled onto the chair

opposite her, the door to the kitchen swung open and William entered the room, carrying two steaming bowls of soup and a plate of biscuits. Like a waiter in an elegant restaurant, he set a bowl in front of each of them, put the plate between them, offered a bow of his head, then retreated into the kitchen.

Tears welled in Amanda's eyes. "We're forgiven, I think."

"Or at the very least, we've been offered a gift of grace."

She nodded.

"Shall we give thanks?" he asked.

"Yes, please."

They bowed their heads, and Isaiah began, "Lord, we thank You for the grace You shed upon us each day. We thank You for the friends who prepared this meal for us to enjoy." He paused.

Amanda lifted her eyes to look at him across the table, but his head remained bowed.

"And Father, I thank You for my wife. Help us to honor You in the way we live. In Your Son's name, we pray. Amen."

Emotions swirling in her chest—hope, trepidation, yearning, love—Amanda dipped her spoon into the golden amber soup and brought it to her mouth. The creamy flavor of butternut squash with just a hint of nutmeg burst on her tongue. "Oh, my. Mr. Kincaid has outdone himself."

"Indeed."

She reached for one of the buttermilk biscuits and slathered the flaky insides with butter. Grateful she wasn't wearing a snug-fitting gown, she took a bite of the warm biscuit. It seemed to melt in her mouth. "Do you realize," she said after swallowing, "that Mr. Kincaid must have planned this meal from the moment he learned we were to wed?"

The goodness of these people overwhelmed her. She'd disappointed them, and still they had planned this evening for her, for them.

A short while later, William returned with the main course—roasted venison, served with a rich blackberry sauce; baked sliced potatoes layered with cream, butter, and a sprinkle of cheese and browned on top; and caramelized carrots.

"William," she said before he could depart, "how did Mr. Kincaid manage to do this for us? He had so little time to plan."

He chuckled. "Don't ask me. The news of your wedding brought out the chef in him, I guess."

"Thank him for us, please. And thank you for your part in it."

He nodded as he pointed to her plate. "Enjoy." He looked at Isaiah. "Both of you."

For a short while, the only sound in the dining room was of utensils clicking on china. The food was every bit as good as she'd anticipated. No, even better. The venison had been perfectly seasoned with herbs, and the brown sugar glazing on the carrots made them taste more like dessert than a vegetable.

"They love you," Isaiah said, his voice low.

She looked up from her plate, desperately wanting to ask if he loved her too. "I know," she whispered at last.

He cleared his throat. "Amanda, I'm sorry you didn't get the kind of wedding you deserve."

"But I shall always treasure the one we had."

"Will you?"

"Yes."

Doubt flickered in his eyes.

After placing her knife and fork on her plate, Amanda leaned forward. "Isaiah Coltrane, do you wish to make me angry, the way you did the night of the barn dance?"

Surprise replaced doubt, and he shook his head.

"Good." She picked up her utensils again. "Then let us enjoy this meal. I'm quite certain we shall not have another like it any time soon."

———

AMANDA HAD NEVER LOOKED MORE beautiful than she did that evening, seated across the table from Isaiah, bathed in flickering candlelight. Beautiful and sweet and innocent. She had no idea how harsh and cruel the world could be. She'd been sheltered and protected by wealth and class. Would his decision to marry her destroy the happiness she felt now? He said another silent prayer against that result.

William, still playing the role of waiter, came to clear the table, returning to the kitchen with the dirty dishes. When he appeared again, he carried a cake on a platter, and he was followed by Chuck and Mrs. Adler. He set the cake on the table, then took a step back.

"It's spiced apple," Chuck said. "I hope you like it, Miss Amanda."

"I will love it, Mr. Kincaid, as I have loved the entire meal. I have never eaten anything more delicious in my life." She leaned slightly toward the cake. "Mmm. I can smell the cinnamon and cloves."

The cook beamed.

"We want to wish you both much happiness," Mrs. Adler said.

Isaiah suspected her good wishes did not come without effort. "Thank you, Mrs. Adler. Thank you all."

The threesome nodded, then disappeared once more into the kitchen.

Amanda rose from the chair and cut the cake, placing the slices on two small plates from the sideboard. Before she could hand one of the plates to him, he found himself standing as well, not sure how it happened. He stood right next to her. Almost touching but not quite.

She tipped her head to gaze up at him, and he did what he'd longed to do all day. He kissed her, and the knowledge that she was his wife, that there was no one but Amanda herself who could stop him from kissing her, caused heat to surge through him. He thought of sweeping her feet off the floor and carrying her across the snowy barnyard to the cottage, of allowing his passion free rein, of showing her the depth of feelings he didn't know how to express, was afraid to express. But he couldn't. He might live like a mountain man, but he would try to always be a gentleman with the lady who had deigned to marry him.

Somehow he called forth enough willpower to end the kiss and take a small step back from her. Emotions swirled in her eyes. Tenderly, he reached out and stroked her cheek.

"Isaiah?"

"Hmm."

"I . . . I don't think I want any cake. Not tonight."

Desire swept through him. "I don't either." His voice sounded gruff in his own ears.

"Perhaps we should go . . . home."

"Home?"

"To the cottage."

He searched her eyes. Did she have any notion what she did to him with that simple suggestion? Did she understand all that marriage entailed?

"Isaiah?"

"Hmm."

"I am not afraid."

"I am," he whispered. Then he swept her feet off the floor, just as he'd wanted to do moments before. Holding her close, he carried her out of the house.

Chapter Twenty-Seven

29 October 1895

Dearest Sebastian and Jocelyn,

I am aware that William sent a telegram last
week with the news of my marriage to Isaiah
Coltrane, but I must write to share my happiness
with you both. I want to say more than can be
stated in a telegram, even though I know the letter
will not reach you quickly.

The ceremony took place in the church in
Gibeon with Reverend Blankenship administering
the vows. It was a simple affair. Mrs. Adler stood up
with me, and that evening Mr. Kincaid prepared us
the most wonderful wedding supper.

Please, dear brother, do not be angry with me
for marrying without waiting for your blessing. I
understand that you have never met Isaiah, that
you had no opportunity to know him and to learn
his character. But I know him. He is a good man.

He is gentle and kind, a man of faith and integrity.
I may also say that he is a man of hidden talents.
Something I did not know before we were wed and
sharing the Eden's Gate guest cottage is that,
although he is a man of the wild and of nature, he
also has talent as a writer. For about a decade, he
has chronicled the stories of mountain men of the
American West. He wrote down these stories for
himself, but I believe they should be published so
others can read them. Perhaps I will convince him
of it one day.

Our future plans are uncertain. For the winter,
Isaiah is working for William on Eden's Gate. But
he owns land in Montana. There is a cabin, but he
says it is not suited for a wife at this time and states
there is much work to be done before we can make
it our home. Isaiah has worked for several years as
a game scout in Yellowstone National Park. I antici-
pate he will want to return to that work when the
snow melts and he is ready for us to relocate to
Montana.

Sebastian, please do not worry about me. I am
where I was always meant to be, although I did not
always know it. You may not believe me, but my
steps were ordained by God. My one regret is that I
may never see you and Jocelyn or Adam and Eliza
again. I may never see my nieces or nephews, and
you may never see yours. While that is a hard truth,
it does not change my certainty that meeting Isaiah,
that marrying him, is just as it should be. I love
him, far more than even he knows.

Your loving sister,
Amanda

Clutching sealed envelopes close to her coat—one addressed to Sebastian, another to Adam, as well as several to friends back in England—Amanda leaned into the icy wind and hurried across the barnyard to the main house. "Mrs. Adler?" she called as she entered through the front door.

The housekeeper appeared out of the hallway leading to William's study. "Yes, Miss Amanda?"

"Do you know if anyone is going into Gibeon today?"

"Afraid not. I heard Mr. William say the men were riding to the south pastures today."

"I see. Well then, I suppose I shall go into town myself."

"Alone, miss?" Poor Mrs. Adler. She would never approve of Amanda's independent ways. But neither had she approved of the same thing in Jocelyn or, from what Amanda had been told, in Jocelyn's mother.

"I have ridden into town alone before, Mrs. Adler. Several times. Today the sky is clear, and Ebony would love a good gallop. So would I." She didn't mention how the hours dragged when Isaiah was away from her. Going into Gibeon was the perfect way to make time speed up again.

"It's awfully cold out, Miss Amanda."

"I shall dress warmly." She turned toward the door.

"Thank you." She gave a small wave of her fingers as she left.

In the cottage, she did as promised, changing into warmer clothing. Afterward, she placed a knit scarf over her head and ears and tied it securely beneath her chin. Then she drew on the heavy winter coat and gloves that Jocelyn had given her before leaving for England. "You'll need these," her sister-in-law had said. Amanda was thankful now for Jocelyn's thoughtfulness.

Smiling at the memory, she headed outside again, this time with her letters tucked safely into a leather saddlebag. Ebony whinnied and trotted over to the fence of the smaller paddock.

"Ready for a run?" She stroked the young mare's head. "Of course you are."

She led Ebony into the barn to saddle and bridle her. While the morning temperature was above freezing, the wind blowing from the west made it feel much colder. Despite that, she was more than ready for this ride. She hoped it would blow away doubts and make some things clearer in her mind.

She hadn't lied in her letter to Sebastian. She *was* happy. When she and Isaiah were alone in the cottage at night, lying in bed, his arms wrapped around her, she thought she might die from sheer bliss. And yet, there was a sliver of sorrow mixed in for he had never declared his love. He showed her in so many ways that he cared. She didn't doubt it was true. But she longed to hear him declare his feelings, and his silence in that regard hurt more than she cared to admit. Worse, it kept her silent as well.

With a shake of her head, she placed her foot in the stirrup and mounted Ebony. The horse pranced eagerly as Amanda settled into the saddle. "Easy, girl."

Moments later, she rode out of the barn and turned the mare toward Gibeon, keeping the horse at a walk for a couple of minutes before allowing her to break into a trot and finally into a canter. The snow from the previous week's storms was gone from the road, but it clung to the northern slopes and shaded areas.

As she'd hoped, the ride—and the cold air—began to clarify her thoughts.

"I've told others I love him. I need to tell him what I feel." She sat a little straighter in the saddle. "I *will* tell him. I'll tell him tonight. I don't need him to speak first. I know my own mind. I know my own heart. I don't have to wait."

Joy, along with a sense of freedom, surged through her, and she leaned lower, asking for more speed from Ebony. The mare obliged, her lengthy strides closing the distance to Gibeon.

Later, when she dismounted outside the general store, her cheeks and nose were numb from the cold. So were her toes and fingertips. When she opened the door, a bell chiming, she thanked God for the heat emanating from the potbelly stove in a corner, and she moved toward it as if drawn by a magnet.

"Land o' Goshen. Is that you, Miss Whitcombe?" Standing behind the counter, Margaret Hathaway gave her head a shake. "I mean, Mrs. Coltrane."

Amanda turned her back to the stove but didn't move away from it. "It's me."

"What on earth brought you all this way on such a cold morning?"

She held the saddlebags away from her body. "I have some letters to mail. But they can wait until I thaw a little."

Margaret laughed. "You do that. I'll be right here when you're ready to post them." The woman looked toward another area of the shop. "Can I help you, sir?"

Amanda couldn't see the other customer because of the tall shelves that blocked her view, but she heard him answer, "No, ma'am. Thanks kindly."

As she moved the saddlebags onto her left shoulder, she turned to face the potbelly stove again. The numbness had begun to ease but wasn't gone yet. She wiggled her fingers before tugging off her gloves, then held her hands, palms out, closer to the stove. The silence in the store was broken only by the sounds of the crackling fire. The cold had kept most shoppers at home apparently. No wonder Margaret had been surprised to see her.

The bell over the doorway chimed again, but when Amanda turned she didn't see a new customer, only the back of the man who had exited the store as he followed the boardwalk in the direction of the feed store.

"Ready for me to post those now?" Margaret asked. "If I get 'em into the mail pouch, they'll be out of here on this afternoon's coach."

"Oh, yes. That would be wonderful." She hurried across the store.

"We were all mighty surprised to learn of your marriage. Guess I told you that on Sunday after church." Margaret watched as Amanda took the envelopes from the bag and laid them on the counter. "But if I didn't say it then, we sure do wish you much happiness."

"Thank you."

"We hope we'll get to know Mr. Coltrane better."

"I hope so too."

"I didn't see much of him at the barbecue and dance."

"No, his ankle didn't allow him to get around much that night."

"Mr. Overstreet told us the cattle rustlers were caught because of Mr. Coltrane's tracking skills."

"Yes, that's true."

"You must be very proud of him." Even as she talked, Margaret took care of the letters on the counter and soon they were in the mail pouch, ready to be sent on their way to England. "Now that your business is done, would you care to sit and have a cup of tea before you face the cold again. In fact, why don't you have lunch with me and my mister."

"That sounds lovely, Mrs. Hathaway. Thank you. I will."

By the time Amanda bid the Hathaways goodbye, her heart was as full as her stomach. She'd known Margaret Hathaway for five months, but today it seemed the woman had become her friend. And in only a few more hours, she could share all about it with

Isaiah. Her trip into town had achieved the very thing she'd wanted the most—to speed up the passage of time.

The sky that had been clear and blue that morning was now covered in a layer of gray clouds. It looked to her as if it might snow, but she was not the best judge of weather. Still, she would hurry Ebony toward home, just in case.

She'd ridden for about fifteen minutes when she saw the man on horseback. Still a good distance off, he raised his arm to draw her attention. Her gut clenched. She didn't know why. It was more than that he was a stranger. Many people in the area remained strangers to her.

"Excuse me, ma'am," he called as she drew closer to him. "Can you point me the way to Eden's Gate? I'm looking for Mr. William Overstreet."

Turn back to town. She silenced the small voice in her head. She wanted to get home to Isaiah. Riding back to town would only delay seeing him.

"You are on the right road, sir."

He was a scruffy looking fellow, badly in need of both a haircut and a shave, and his coat didn't appear to offer sufficient warmth against the frigid temperature.

"Are you looking for work?" she asked him.

"Yes, ma'am."

The tension inside her eased a bit. She didn't want to judge someone simply because they were down on their luck, and the man had been nothing but polite. "I am headed to Eden's Gate myself. You are welcome to ride along if you like."

"I would like, ma'am. Thanks kindly." He turned his horse and fell in beside her.

They rode in silence, Amanda's thoughts returning to Isaiah and how much she enjoyed watching him shave in the mornings. Who would have thought watching such a simple act could be so … sensual. She smiled as the image from that morning played in her mind, Isaiah wearing his trousers but no shirt, leaning over the bowl, his gaze locked on the mirror as he ran the razor blade over his cheek. His hair had still been disheveled, and she'd thought to rise from the bed to run her fingers through it. But the bedroom had still been cold, and so she'd stayed beneath the blankets and simply enjoyed the view.

The stranger fell back slightly and as she turned to speak to him, movement from the side caught her attention an instant before something hard smacked her in the back of her head. She swayed, grasping for the saddle horn. But it was too late. She was already toppling from the saddle as blackness enveloped her.

THERE WASN'T a man among William's ranch hands who wasn't eager to finish this work day a couple of hours earlier than usual. It had been a day spent fighting a frigid wind as they drove cattle from the southern part of the range closer to the ranch complex, and all the cowboys looked forward to some time beside a warm fire. Isaiah knew the temperatures would only continue to drop in the coming weeks, but it wasn't the promise of warmth that made him yearn to get back home. He simply wanted to return to his bride.

Beneath the knit scarf wrapped around the lower half of his face, he grinned. A week married and completely besotted. Turned out, being caught with Amanda in the cottage by Mrs. Adler had been the best thing that ever happened to him. Would he have married her otherwise? He didn't think so. Certainly not so quickly. More likely he would have saddled Buck, called for Bandit, and ridden back to Montana, telling himself he was doing her a favor, convinced that he wasn't good enough to be her husband. But now that he *was* her husband, all that was left for him to do was become a better man. A man truly worthy of her.

With his head bent into the wind, he didn't see the ranch house come into view. It was the quickening of Buck's pace that told him they were close. He glanced up, his gaze fastening on the roof of the cottage. Home . . . and Amanda. He pressed his heels into his horse's sides.

The men were dismounting outside the barn when Mrs. Adler scurried out of the house, clutching a shawl around her shoulders. She made a beeline for him, and he wondered what he'd done wrong.

"Mr. Coltrane, I'm so glad you're back."

He looked at her, surprised by her choice of words.

"It's Miss Amanda. Something's happened."

Alarm shot through him, and he spun toward the cottage.

"No! She's not there. She's . . . she's missing."

He turned back to the housekeeper. "Missing?"

William stepped up beside him. "What happened, Mrs. Adler?"

"I don't know. She rode into town this morning on that spotted horse of hers. She said she had letters to mail and she wanted to go for a ride so would take them herself."

"And?" Isaiah prompted.

"Well, she was gone a long time. A lot longer than what I expected. Then about an hour ago, her horse came back all by itself. Mr. Flores was here by then. He'd come back from fixing a fence or something. He saw her horse trot right up to the barn, reins dragging the ground. We knew right away something wasn't right, of course. So he went to look for her, and he hasn't returned. I don't know if he's found her or what's happened."

Isaiah grabbed the saddle horn and swung onto Buck's back. He whistled for Bandit but didn't say a word to the others before spinning the horse away from them. He had Buck at a gallop before they rounded the barn.

Fear gripped him, and his heart hammered. Only a short while ago he'd been smiling at the thought of returning to Amanda at the end of the day. And now she was missing? She must have been thrown. Was she lying somewhere hurt, unconscious?

Father in heaven, help me find her. Keep her safe.

He heard horses' hooves pounding the hard ground and knew William and his men followed after him. Bandit would be not far behind, although the dog couldn't keep up at this pace. Not for long anyway. But hopefully they wouldn't have far to go. Hopefully they would come upon Tom Flores and Amanda at any moment. But when Tom finally came into view, he was alone on his horse.

Isaiah reined in. "Any sign of Amanda?"

"No, sir." The cowboy shook his head. "I rode all the way into town. Found out she had lunch with the Hathaways, then started back to the ranch. Mrs. Hathaway saw her riding in this direction."

From behind Isaiah, William said, "All right. Spread out men. If there's no sign of her along the road, she must have ridden off it for some reason. We don't have but a few hours until dark. We need to find her before then."

Please, God. Make it so.

Chapter Twenty-Eight

Amanda blinked. An instant later, pain exploded in her head, and she closed her eyes again. But not before she'd seen a fire flickering in a fireplace on the opposite side of a room.

But what room? Where was she?

It returned to her, slowly. The man on the road from Gibeon, asking her the way to Eden's Gate. Something striking her on the back of her head. The fall from the saddle.

Bracing for more pain, she opened her eyes a second time. She blinked, waiting for her vision to adjust to the dim light. She had no idea how long she'd been unconscious, how long they'd traveled to get to this place. She had a faint memory of coming to and finding herself belly down across the back of a horse. But she must have fainted again because she remembered nothing else after that.

She inhaled slowly and quietly, trying to make sense of her surroundings. She lay on blankets on the floor, her hands and feet bound. Near the fireplace, her assailant sat in a straight-backed chair, eating something out of a can. She saw him in silhouette, elbows on his thighs as he dipped a spoon into the can, then brought it to his lips.

Stifling a groan, she pushed herself to a sitting position.

He caught the movement and looked toward her. "You've come to at last. Good. You wouldn't be any use to me dead."

"What do you want with me?" Her head throbbed, and she winced. "Who are you?"

"Listen to you. All high and mighty. I don't got to tell you nothing."

"What is your name?"

"You don't need to know it. But I know yours, Mrs. Coltrane. I surely know yours."

The way he said it sent a shiver up her spine. "If it's a ransom you want, you're wasting your time. My husband is not a wealthy man."

He dropped the tin can and spoon on the floor. "Makes no difference. It's not money I'm after." He stood and took a step in her direction. His face was hidden in shadows, the light of the fire behind him.

She shivered again.

"They said they would never have found us if it weren't for Coltrane."

"Found who?"

"And my brother wouldn't be dead either."

She shook her head slowly. His words made no sense.

"But if Coltrane's as good at trackin' as they say, then I reckon he can find you. And when he comes, I'll be waitin' for him."

Amanda didn't know who this man was. She knew nothing about his brother or why her kidnapper blamed Isaiah. But she knew what he meant to do. He meant to kill her husband, and he meant to use her to do it.

Father, help us!

She drew a steadying breath. "Sir, I need to use the outhouse."

He grunted.

"Please."

He took another step toward her, and she felt his gaze study her. At last he said, "All right."

She held out her arms. "You'll need to untie my wrists."

He grunted a second time before closing the remaining distance between them. It took some time for him to free the knot. After the rope fell away, she rubbed one wrist, then the other, not realizing until then how the rough cord had chafed her skin. Then she leaned forward and untied the rope around her ankles.

"I'll be watchin' you. You try to run, and I'll shoot you dead. Hear me?"

"I won't run." She pushed herself up from the floor, her head pounding, her body stiff and sore. "I give you my word." Even as she made the promise, she knew she'd break it if the opportunity arose.

Her captor picked up a rifle before moving to the door and opening it. "Don't forget. I'm watchin'."

After the dim light of the cabin, she was surprised to

find there was still lingering daylight outside. She looked around, located the outhouse, and walked in that direction, noting the trees and the snow on the ground. While she had been slung across a horse unconscious, they must have covered considerable distance, carrying them to a higher elevation. But had they gone north or west? Where was Eden's Gate from here? If she managed to escape, she wouldn't know what direction to run, and she'd never survive a night in these mountains.

"Hurry up," the man called as she opened the outhouse door. "It's cold out here."

A short while later, she began the return walk to the cabin. Both sky and earth had turned to shades of gray by this time, and she could see little of the surrounding terrain. She re-entered the cabin fearing she hadn't learned anything of value.

"May I warm myself by the fire?" She affected a shiver.

He motioned with the rifle. "Go ahead."

She sat on the chair he'd vacated earlier and held her hands toward the fire. She remembered doing the same thing in the mercantile, warming her cold hands by the potbelly stove. How many hours ago had that been? It seemed another lifetime, but at most it had been seven hours or so. Isaiah would have returned to the ranch long before now. He and the others would realize she was missing, but they wouldn't know she'd been taken by a stranger with a grudge against Isaiah.

But her husband was a tracker. If anyone could find her it was him. Her heart skittered. He would find her, but he wouldn't know he rode into a trap.

God, protect him.

Darkness overtook Isaiah, William, and Tom, making it impossible for them to follow the single horse's tracks any longer. They were forced to make camp for the night. Thankfully, Logan Coe and Jake Foster caught up with them before too long, bringing supplies from the ranch that they would need that night and the next day. God forbid that the search took longer than that.

Isaiah usually worked alone when tracking, but in this case, he was glad others had volunteered to join him. He didn't know who he tracked or what they would find when they caught up with him. Amanda's kidnapper was a lone rider now, but there might be a plan to join others.

Isaiah knew for certain they followed a man. The culprit had left his large bootprints in the snow near where they'd found Amanda's saddlebags and signs of a scuffle. He didn't want to think what that might mean, but at least there hadn't been any blood in the snow.

As firelight flickered across the men's faces, they ate jerky and hard rolls and sipped coffee from tin cups, their shoulders hunched against the falling temperature. He shuddered to think of Amanda out there in this cold.

"You doing all right?" William asked softly.

Isaiah looked up at the sky. There were no stars. The heavens were hidden by clouds. "Not really."

"She's smart. She'll be okay."

"Who would take her? And why?"

"Don't know."

Another question rolled in his head. One he couldn't give voice to. What was Amanda's captor doing to her while Isaiah sat beside a campfire, waiting for daylight? The question felt as if it would crush him. He closed his eyes and said a silent prayer for protection for her.

Chapter Twenty-Nine

They left the cabin as the sun rose above the mountain range in the east, Amanda seated on a horse provided by her kidnapper, although she had no control over it. Her hands were tightly bound once again, and her captor held tightly to the lead rope. For the hundredth time, she prayed that Ebony had made it back to the ranch safely.

It was tempting to try kicking the horse into action, but she knew nothing of this mount's nature and didn't trust it. Besides, she knew any attempt to escape would be useless. Even if she yanked the man out of his saddle, it wouldn't take him long to catch her.

No, she had to be smart. First, she would watch and pray. Somewhere behind them, Isaiah searched for her. She would be ready when he came. And she would do her best to protect him from whatever his enemy had in store.

With her eyes studying the terrain, she turned her heart toward heaven and asked God to clothe her in His full armor. She asked Him to do the same for Isaiah. She prayed for wisdom and for courage. Remembering words from the fifth Psalm, she asked God to destroy the enemy by his own counsel.

Her gaze returned to the man on the horse in front of her. "Let him fall into his own trap, Lord. Let his plans turn against him."

He looked over his shoulder at her with a scowl.

Make him afraid, Father. Fill him with fear of his own making.

As soon as he turned forward again, she used pressure from her leg to move her mount closer to the underbrush growing alongside the trail, trying to knock off the snow and break as many small branches as possible with her boot. As long as it didn't snow again, these signs would linger, and Isaiah would find them.

Warn Isaiah, God. Let him know this man means to trap him.

Through a break in the low-slung clouds, she caught sight of the Tetons off to her right, far in the distance. That meant they were headed northeast. Did he mean to take them into Yellowstone? Was that his destination?

She had her answer around midday when they arrived at another cabin, this one more ramshackle than the first.

"Get down," the man ordered. He waited to dismount until she obeyed.

Her legs wobbled underneath her, and she gripped the stirrup to steady herself. She was tired, hungry, and thirsty. And her toes and fingers were numb from the cold.

"Get inside."

Her heart screamed for her to run. Her head told her there was no place to hide. There were only a few trees here and little underbrush.

Watch and pray, a voice whispered in her head.

Once inside the cabin, her captor bound her to a chair, then retreated outdoors. From the noise he made, she guessed he was corralling the horses in the small pen she'd noticed on the backside of the cabin. When he returned, he stomped the snow off his boots, then squatted on the hearth and built a fire.

"Is this your cabin?" she asked.

"Suppose so. Me and my brother used it plenty enough the last few years."

"Used it when?"

He swiveled toward her. "Curious one, ain't you?"

"You waylaid me on the road for a reason I don't understand. You seem to know my husband and blame him for something that happened to your brother. Of course I'm curious. I don't even know who you are. I don't know your name."

"Hmm." He rubbed his grizzled chin between thumb and forefinger. "Well, I don't reckon it matters if I tell you what you want to know."

Her pulse raced, understanding what that meant. He didn't intend for her to leave this cabin with whatever information he gave her. He meant to kill Isaiah, and then he would kill her, too.

"Name's Perkins. My brother and me, we come down from Montana last summer, riding with some other men, and we helped ourselves to a few cattle off some of the ranches. Not so much most of those rich men should even bother with."

"You're a cattle thief?"

He glared at her. "We weren't hurtin' nobody. A man's got to live."

She pressed her lips together. A thief was a thief, but she wouldn't tell him so.

"We would've got away with it, too, like we done before. And then they brought in a tracker. That's how they found our place in Montana. That's how they got my brother. Coltrane caused it."

"Isaiah didn't go to Montana, Mr. Perkins. An injury kept him in Idaho. A broken ankle. He was at the ranch when they arrested the rustlers."

"Maybe he wasn't in Montana, but he's the one who found the trail we used all summer long. Nobody else ever thought to go that high up the mountains. It was Coltrane who found the trail. I heard lawmen talkin' about it later."

She drew a breath and released it, trying to keep her voice steady and soft. "What happened to your brother?"

"He got hisself shot dead, tryin' to escape."

"I'm sorry he's dead, but that's not Isaiah's fault."

Perkins moved so fast, she had no time to brace herself before he backhanded her. Her head snapped to the side, and pain exploded inside her head once again. Tears welled in her eyes.

"You think it matters to me if he was there or not?" He ground out the question. "He put the law on our trail, and my brother's dead. I come back to Idaho to make him pay for it. It was just my luck you come into the mercantile yesterday. I heard your name. Mrs. Coltrane." He practically spit the words. "And I knew right then how I was gonna make him come to me so I could get my revenge."

Amanda blinked away the tears. "You plan to be a murderer and a thief?"

He looked as if he might hit her again, but he stopped himself, then revealed a cruel smile. "Yeah, and you get to watch me do it."

———

Isaiah and the other men came upon the cabin mid-morning. There were no horses in the small corral, but there had been. And recently. Two of them, judging by the prints left on the ground.

While the others searched the area, Isaiah and William went inside the cabin. The first thing Isaiah saw was the smoldering remains of a fire. An empty can of beans lay close to the hearth. Moments later, Isaiah found a handkerchief tucked between the folds of a blanket on the floor. A handkerchief embroidered with Amanda's initials.

"We're on the right trail," he said to William, holding up the handkerchief for him to see.

"Didn't doubt we were." He nodded. "I'd guess she left that for you on purpose."

"I reckon the same."

He put the handkerchief into the pocket of his coat,

his heart hammering. She'd trusted that he was in hot pursuit, and the knowledge comforted him.

As he and William exited the cabin, the three other men joined them.

"We covered a lot of ground this morning," Isaiah said. "Whoever's got Amanda isn't traveling as fast as we are."

William frowned. "Something feels off to me."

"What do you mean?"

"Why did this man, whoever he is, make it obvious that they stayed in this cabin last night? He could have covered his tracks better." With a gesture, William indicated Isaiah's coat pocket. "He could have made sure Amanda left no clues."

"Maybe he isn't very smart," Logan said with a shrug.

Isaiah fingered the handkerchief in his pocket. "No. William's right. He could have done more to make it difficult for us to find them." He looked in the direction Amanda and her captor had gone. "Seems like he might be luring us in. We need to keep that in mind."

Keep it in mind, he would, but he wouldn't let it slow him down. He knew how to be fast and careful at the same time.

———

AMANDA'S HEAD continued to throb. Despite the fire, she was cold as well as tired, hungry, and thirsty, and she could taste blood on her tongue. She assumed when Perkins hit her he'd split her lip. But none of those things mattered to her. All that mattered was getting free of the ropes that bound her.

Her captor hadn't been as careful when he pushed her onto this chair and tied her ankles to the chair legs and her hands behind her back. The ropes were not as snug as they'd been yesterday. Perhaps he was as tired as she was and was getting careless because of it.

Perkins had positioned a second chair near the only window in yet another one-room cabin. The window faced the deep clearing they'd ridden across. No one could cross it without being seen. Not in the daylight. As she watched, Perkins leaned two loaded rifles against the wall. Then he checked the chambers of the two revolvers.

With the coarse rope scraping her skin, she slid her right hand a little closer to freedom. Every movement she made, she feared Perkins would notice, but he didn't. His focus remained on the view out that window. It was obvious he expected Isaiah to come for her soon.

She believed the same. He couldn't be far away. Thirty minutes. An hour. Two hours. However long it took, he was coming. But Perkins was waiting. Perkins was laying a trap, and she couldn't let Isaiah fall into it.

She twisted her hands again and pulled against the rope. Her right hand came free so suddenly she tipped sideways, almost falling from the chair. She righted herself before Perkins's head jerked toward her.

"Sit still."

"I'm sorry. I'm just so tired. I . . . I started to fall asleep."

His gaze narrowed.

Dread iced through her. Did he believe what she'd claimed? Would he come over to check her bindings? But he didn't. He turned his eyes out the window once again.

Keeping her hands behind her back, she wiggled her left wrist and the rope slipped to the seat of the chair. Now, to figure out how to free her ankles. After making sure Perkins's attention remained on the clearing beyond the window, she leaned slightly forward and looked down. Her riding skirt was long enough to hide the ropes that bound her. If she could untie them but her skirt remained as it was now, he wouldn't know that she'd freed herself. But how to do that?

Watch and pray. Those were the words that kept coming to her. Those were the words she would obey.

Lord, blind him. Cover his eyes with scales so he cannot see.

As if in answer, Perkins got up from his chair. He glanced in her direction at the same time he grabbed one rifle. "Sit still and be quiet." He went to the door, cracked it open, waited a short while, then went outside.

Holding her breath, she leaned forward and began working to untie the knots.

Chapter Thirty

I saiah smiled grimly when he saw more broken
branches. Amanda's captor wasn't being careful to
hide their tracks, but he would wager good money that
she was the one leaving the evidence of their passing.

"We're close," he said. "I feel it in my gut."

William nodded.

Raising his voice slightly, he said, "Keep your eyes
peeled. He's waiting for us, and he may not be alone any
longer. He may have companions with him by now. And
don't forget. He's got Amanda. We don't want to put her
at risk."

He steeled his nerves against the images his warning
brought to mind. Until Amanda entered his life, Isaiah
hadn't had another person to put before himself. Not
since the death of his father. He hadn't needed to be
afraid for anyone's safety or good health or happiness.
Letting Amanda into his heart, loving her as he did, had
changed everything.

Up ahead, Bandit froze, his body crouched low.

Isaiah raised a hand as he reined in. The other men obeyed the silent command. He slid from the saddle and took his rifle from its scabbard. With a few hand motions, he showed his intent to circle around to the north. Then he and Bandit moved through the trees, alert to the surrounding sounds. Minutes later, he spotted the cabin, two horses in a corral behind it. A large clearing surrounded the building and pen. It would be impossible for anyone to approach from the front without being seen. There was one window near the door on the front but none on the side closest to him. He moved silently on, keeping his eye on the cabin while he stuck to the cover of the forest. Bandit stayed close by, ready to follow any command Isaiah might give.

His heart sank when he saw there were no other windows. He hadn't expected another door in such a small, simple cabin, but another window would have been welcome. As it was, he could sneak up to the back of the log house without being seen. He could then sidle around to the front. But how could he get inside without putting Amanda in danger? He didn't know where she was. Near the door? Near the window? Near the fireplace? He couldn't be certain if she was even inside, although it was unlikely the kidnapper had hidden her elsewhere. He would have seen those tracks.

He completed the circuit around the cabin to where the other men waited for him. Quickly, he described what he'd discovered.

"He's gotta be in there, and he's waiting for us," he finished.

William nodded.

Isaiah looked toward the cabin. He couldn't actually see the building from here, but it was clear in his mind. He pictured its size and shape. He pictured the front door and window and visualized the size of the clearing. If the man inside that cabin had been alone, it wouldn't be all that hard for Isaiah and the others to overtake him. One way in or out worked both for and against him. It was the hostage that made the situation dangerous. For Amanda.

An icy rage coiled inside him. Poachers had shot at him more than once in the past. But he'd never felt the urge to kill someone himself until now. If anything happened to Amanda, he wasn't sure what he would do with the man who'd taken her hostage. "We need a plan."

"I say a couple of us keep him occupied from a distance, and the others get closer to the cabin. At some point, he'll run out of food and water. He'll need to sleep or maybe he'll come outside. Then we can rush him."

It wasn't a brilliant plan, but Isaiah couldn't think of a better one. Not yet anyway.

Logan said, "I can draw his fire."

Jake nodded. "Me too."

"And maybe we can take him down," Logan added. "We're both good shots."

"Just make sure you're out of his range," William responded.

"You got it, boss." Jake jerked on his hat brim.

Isaiah looked from William to Tom. "I guess that means you two are coming with me. You can stake out one side of the cabin. Bandit and I'll take the other. Don't make a sound. We don't want him to know how many of us there are."

Taking the request for silence seriously, the two men nodded. Then they moved off through the trees, William and Tom to the north, Isaiah with Bandit to the south.

"You, in the house!"

Amanda's heart leapt at the shout coming from outside.

Perkins shot up from his chair, rifle ready, the side of his head pressed against the wall next to the window frame. "Yeah?"

"We've come for the woman." That was Jake Foster's voice.

"Coltrane?" Perkins shouted back.

"No. He's not with us."

"Don't he care what happens to his wife?" He glanced over his shoulder at Amanda.

She hid a knowing smile. Isaiah was out there. She knew it with every fiber of her being.

"He would care," Jake responded. "But he rode down to Pocatello yesterday. He's not expected back for a few days."

Perkins cursed.

Amanda forced herself to sit still, despite the temptation to bolt for the door. What Jake said was a lie. She knew it, but Perkins didn't.

"Let her go, and we'll just ride away with her. Coltrane doesn't even need to know what you did."

"If he don't know yet, he'll know before this is over." Perkins moved the rifle to a new position. "She's not goin' nowhere until Coltrane comes for her himself. Hear me?"

"We hear you."

"Amanda." Her whispered name was so soft, she feared she'd imagined it. "Amanda." She hadn't imagined it. Isaiah was saying her name. Slowly, she turned her head and noticed for the first time a small gap in the chinking. Isaiah was right outside, speaking to her.

She looked toward her captor again. "Let me go, Mr. Perkins. No one has to get hurt."

"Shut up."

"You can't hold them off forever. It's you against heaven knows how many others. You can't keep me prisoner forever. Just let me go."

"It's only one man I want, and I'll get him before this is over. Now shut up or I'll make you shut up."

Amanda drew a breath, knowing Isaiah had more information now than he'd had moments before. He knew for certain that there was only one man with her in the cabin. He knew her exact location. What he couldn't know was that she'd freed herself, that nothing bound her to this chair. She was ready for whatever would happen next, and she was certain she wouldn't have long to wait. Isaiah was coming to her rescue—not for the first time.

Wait. There was one more thing he needed to know.

Something that couldn't wait until he freed her. Something she wanted him to know now.

"Mr. Perkins?"

"I said shut up." He growled the words.

"I love my husband, and I don't want him to die."

"Don't care what you want, lady. Now be quiet or I'll gag you. Hear me?"

Her pulse stuttered. Who would watch the window if he took the time to gag her? No one, but had he thought of that? It didn't seem so.

"How can I be quiet when I know what your intention is? You may have two rifles and two revolvers, but that won't be enough to hold them off. Not for long. You didn't think this through. Maybe if you hadn't taken me hostage you could have surprised my husband and killed him as you said you want to do. But you can't surprise him now. The men of Eden's Gate know you have me. You will never have a moment to relax. Not as long as you keep me prisoner. This is an impossible situation. You know that by now. You must."

"Shut up!" he shouted, one hand going to his forehead, as if she'd given him a headache.

"You surely must see that I'm right."

Rifle still in one hand, Perkins took a couple of steps toward her, his free hand raised to strike. "I've had enough of you!"

That's when the door to the cabin burst open.

Isaiah didn't have to assess the situation. He knew where Amanda sat in the cabin and had heard the man named Perkins move away from his station at the window, presumably to silence her. That was the moment he'd waited for, crouched outside the door, listening to his wife give him as much information as she could.

He lunged toward her captor, but before he made contact with Perkins, Amanda thrust herself from the chair. Her arms went around the other man's lower legs a second before Isaiah rammed him in the midsection. Perkins hit the floor hard, and the rifle flew from his hand. Isaiah let go and rose to his knees. When Perkins tried to hit him, Bandit joined the fray, biting down on Perkins's wrist. He howled in pain.

"Isaiah?" came William's voice from outside.

"We've got him," he answered as his gaze went to Amanda, who had scrambled to her feet and now held the rifle pointed at Perkins.

William and Tom entered the cabin, guns drawn.

A hint of a smile tipped the corners of her mouth. "You'll find some rope under the chair to tie him with."

"Bandit, release." Isaiah stood, ready to let the other men handle Perkins. He needed to hold his wife. As if reading his mind, she leaned the rifle against the wall and ran into his waiting arms. "Are you all right?" he asked softly. But he didn't wait for her answer before pressing his lips to hers. Moments later, he broke the kiss only long enough to say, "If he hurt you . . ."

William said, "We'll be ready to go when you are, Isaiah." Footsteps told of their departure, with Perkins dragging behind, but neither he nor Amanda looked toward the door.

He ran his thumb across a bruise on her cheek. "He hit you."

"It's nothing. I'm all right. So are you."

"So am I." He kissed the bruise.

"I believed God would protect me, Isaiah, and I knew you would find me. I just needed to be ready so I could help you when the time came."

He released a low chuckle as he shook his head. Their gazes locked. "You are so . . . *unexpected*, my love."

Tears filled her eyes.

"My sweet, sweet love," he whispered before kissing her again.

William and the others could wait.

Chapter Thirty-One

9 December 1895

Dearest Sebastian and Jocelyn,

What joyous news you sent with your last letter! Now I will be an aunt twice over. And how wonderful that your child and Adam's will be so near to each other, both in age and in proximity. I will expect many letters, and you must send photographs too.

After all the excitement that happened in October (I already wrote to you about it), life has settled into a quiet and comfortable routine on the ranch. Isaiah enjoys working with William and the men of Eden's Gate, but he is talking more and more about our return to Montana in the spring. He's begun sketching changes he wants to make to his cabin. <u>Our</u> cabin, although I have yet to see it. He's even mentioned the need to enlarge it for a family.

No, that is not my way of announcing important news. Someday, I hope I will give you an American nephew or niece. Several of them, if we are so blessed. For now, I am content living with Isaiah and learning more about this land I now think of as my home.

Last night, as I drifted off to sleep, I thought again of the Wild West Show that instilled in me the desire to visit America, to see the Palouse horses and the buffalo and the cowboys and the great herds of cattle and all that makes this great land unique and beautiful. While I knew how to live among British society, that life never fit me. But I fit here, and I am so thankful to God for bringing me to Idaho. I am also thankful for the poachers who caused my horse to throw me into a river so that Isaiah could rescue me. And he loves to say that I rescued him right back.

I hope I am sending this letter in time for you to receive it before Christmas. If so, happy Christmas to everyone at Hooke Manor. Know that I am thinking of you and sending my love to you all. If not, then I will take this moment to wish you all the happiest of new years. May 1896 be a blessed year for our entire family.

Your loving sister,
Amanda

Epilogue

Yellowstone National Park, late June 1896

I saiah dismounted and squatted to get a better look at the tracks left in the earth.

"How many horses?" Amanda asked softly.

"Six, I think. Four with riders. Two pack horses. I'd say they passed by here four or five hours ago."

She dismounted too. "How can you tell?"

He hid a smile. She was like this, his wife. Curious about everything. Always inquisitive and eager to learn.

"Look here." He trailed a finger over the ground. "Each horse leaves a unique print. Shape and size, shod or unshod. They're moving in a line, single file, and you can see slight variations in the spacing of each horse's stride." He pressed his finger into one print. "This print is deeper. The horse is carrying more weight. Meaning it's likely packing supplies. And the tracks are fresh. Still distinct. Not much time or weather to erode them. Which means they were here this morning."

"You see all that?"

"Every track has its own shape and story. Once you know what to look for, the rest becomes second nature." He stood and turned toward her.

Much of Amanda's head was hidden beneath a floppy brown hat, but he knew she'd braided her hair that morning into a thick, single plait that hung down her back beneath her coat. She had replaced her split riding skirt with trousers, and although her friends back in England would undoubtedly be scandalized by her attire, he thought she looked perfect. Too perfect maybe, because now all he wanted to do was kiss her instead of track poachers.

Bandit came to stand between the two of them. As if to keep them from kissing, he pushed first on Isaiah's legs, then on Amanda's. She laughed lightly, and— perhaps because they weren't far from the river—he recalled the first time he'd heard that delightful sound. That was when he decided the poachers could wait.

He swept her feet off the ground and held her close to his chest.

"Isaiah, what are you doing?"

"I thought you were about to faint."

"Don't be ridiculous. I would not faint."

"You've fainted before." He moved his lips closer to hers. "And I carried you, just like this."

Her voice deepened. "Not *just* like this." She wrapped her arms around his neck and drew his head down. Their lips met, and heat coiled through him, as it always did when she kissed him that way. With love. With abandon. With a promise of forever on her lips.

As had happened often over recent months, he marveled at the changes in his life. Only God Himself could have brought this amazing woman all the way from England to Idaho, then sent her to Yellowstone National Park so she could fall into a river and be pulled from the rushing water by an unsuspecting game scout.

He may have rescued her, but she'd captured him. And he would be forever thankful that she had.

If you enjoyed *To Capture a Mountain Man*, please take a moment to leave a review on Goodreads, BookBub, and/or your favorite retailer.

The British Are Coming

THE BRITISH ARE COMING series begins with *To Enchant a Lady's Heart*, a novella set in Victorian England. It continues with three novels set in America in the mid-1890s featuring Sebastian Whitcombe, heir to the Earl of Hooke; his younger sister, Lady Amanda Whitcombe; and his tradesman friend, Roger Bernhardt. Adventure and romance abound!

TURN THE PAGE FOR A PEEK
AT ROGER'S STORY
COMING IN SUMMER 2025

THE BRITISH ARE COMING
SERIES

TO Reveal
A Reckless Love

Robin Lee
HATCHER

CHRISTY AWARD WINNING AUTHOR

TO REVEAL A RECKLESS LOVE
The British Are Coming, Book 4
Coming Summer 2025
by
Robin Lee Hatcher

———

Roger Bernhardt sees the world as a canvas, yearning to capture nature's splendor with his paintbrush. In Yellowstone National Park, Roger hopes to discover not only inspiration but a future he didn't dare imagine while in England.

Determined and pragmatic, Victoria Castleton has little patience for dreamers like Roger—men who chase beauty instead of stability. Yet, as their paths cross, Victoria finds herself drawn to his vision of the world, a perspective that awakens her to more than the breathtaking wonders around her.

The British Are Coming Series
Books 1 & 2

Return to Kings Meadow in this two novella collection, *From This Moment On*, available in spring 2025

About the Author

Robin Lee Hatcher is the best-selling author of over 95 books. Her well-drawn characters and heartwarming stories of faith, courage, and love have earned her both critical acclaim and the devotion of readers. Her numerous awards include the Christy Award, the RITA® Award, Romantic Times Career Achievement Awards for Americana Romance and for Inspirational Fiction, the Carol Award, and Lifetime Achievement Awards from both Romance Writers of America® (2001) and American Christian Fiction Writers (2014).

When not writing, Robin enjoys being with her family, spending time in the beautiful Idaho outdoors, Bible art journaling, reading books that make her cry, watching romantic movies, knitting, and decorative planning. A mother and grandmother, Robin makes her home on the outskirts of Boise, sharing it with a demanding Papillon dog.

Learn more about Robin and her books and subscribe to her newsletter on her website at robinleehatcher.com

Also by
Robin Lee Hatcher

Stand Alone Titles

Like the Wind

I'll Be Seeing You

Words Matter

Make You Feel My Love

An Idaho Christmas

Here in Hart's Crossing

The Victory Club

Beyond the Shadows

Catching Katie

Whispers From Yesterday

The Shepherd's Voice

Ribbon of Years

Firstborn

The Forgiving Hour

Heart Rings

A Wish and a Prayer

When Love Blooms

A Carol for Christmas

Return to Me

Loving Libby

Wagered Heart

The Perfect Life

Speak to Me of Love

Trouble in Paradise

Another Chance to Love You

Bundle of Joy

The British Are Coming

To Enchant a Lady's Heart

To Marry an English Lord

To Capture a Mountain Man

Boulder Creek Romance

Even Forever

All She Ever Dreamed

The Coming to America Series

Dear Lady

Patterns of Love

In His Arms

Promised to Me

Where the Heart Lives Series

Belonging

Betrayal

Beloved

Books set in Kings Meadow

A Promise Kept

Love Without End

Whenever You Come Around

I Hope You Dance

Keeper of the Stars

Books set in Thunder Creek

You'll Think of Me

You're Gonna Love Me

The Sisters of Bethlehem Springs Series

A Vote of Confidence

Fit to Be Tied

A Matter of Character

Legacy of Faith series

Who I am With You

Cross My Heart

How Sweet It Is

For a full list of books, visit robinlcchatcher.com

.

www.ingramcontent.com/pod-product-compliance
Ingram Content Group UK Ltd.
Pitfield, Milton Keynes, MK11 3LW, UK
UKHW031929310125
454496UK00004B/214

9 781962 005081